Richard Woolley
8/29/20

The Whimple Inn

Written and Illustrated by
Rachel Woolsey

So and So Publishing
146 Mill St.
Springville, NY 14141

1

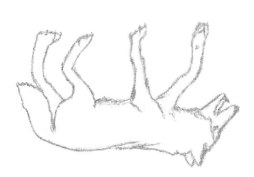

I tripped over a tree root and hit a sharp rock. Bright, yellow stars danced before my eyes. In a numbing pain, I lay sprawled on the ground...

"Are you okay?"

"What?" I mumbled.

Slowly, I opened my eyes and spotted a girl, standing over me. She was around my age, 12.

"Who are you?" I asked. "Where am I?"

"It's alright," she answered. "I'm one of you."

"One of you?"

What does she mean? Glancing around, I saw that it was almost the crack of dawn. *How long have I been out?*

"Yes, you know, a shapeshifter."

"Shapeshifter?"

"Yes, isn't it obvious? I mean, you're…" She pointed. "A wolf."

I gave a low growl. I wasn't sure if it was from anger or from embarrassment. *How humiliating! Now what am I going to do? How am I going to turn back?*

"Wow, this is serious!" said the girl. "My name is Dori Whimple. What's yours?"

"Eddie."

"Okay, well let's get you out of your wolf form."

"How do I do that?"

"It's really simple. Just imagine yourself as a person."

Taking her advice, I tried my best. Eventually, I felt a tingling sensation. And before I knew it, I was on two legs.

"Wow, thanks!" I then searched around. *Oh no! Where are they?*

"What are you looking for?"

"My shoes!"

"I can't really see, but I think they're behind you."

Sure enough, there were my shoes.

"I guess, they fell off when I accidentally transformed." I put my shoes on. "Thanks."

"Don't mention it." She stood there, examining me. At first, she was smiling. But then a funny expression crossed her face. *Was something wrong?*

"What?"

"You're about my age."

"Yeah, so?"

"Nothing, I'm just surprised. That's all... So, what are you doing out here?"

"Running away."

"From who?"

"My uncle, Count Razor."

"Why?"

"Because he's evil. I got landed with him after my family was killed in a terrible car accident."

"That's awful! Does he know you're out here?"

"I thought he was chasing me. It must... have been an animal." My face turned scarlet.

"There's nothing to be embarrassed about. I'd be scared too if I thought someone was trying to kill me."

"I didn't say I was scared." I crossed my arms. I then noticed an odd smell. "Do you smell something?"

"Yeah, it's smoke. Maybe someone's burning brush. In fact, it looks hazy out here. We better go."

"Wait, you didn't tell me what you're doing out here? And how come you don't have a flashlight?"

"How come you don't?"

"Because I'm running away!"

"Well, I'm honing my skills," she said, raising her nose in the air. "I didn't want to attract attention."

"So, your parents don't know you're out here?"

"No. But you're not going to tell on me, are you?"

"I guess not. So, how did you know that I was a... uh?"

"Shapeshifter. I have a way of FEELING things."

"Really?"

"Actually, it was because you were upside down. I've never seen a wolf with its legs sticking in the air like that. Plus, I can read your mind. All shapeshifters can communicate telepathically."

My face turned red again.

"I can see you didn't know that. Technically, you're a shapeshifter, because it's in your genes. It's passed down from your parents to you."

"But my parents were normal."

"Which means they must have been carriers. Come on, you're coming with me!"

2

I trailed after Dori. I still had a lot of questions to ask. I wanted to know if I could trust her.

"Where are we going?"

"To my house."

"Your house?"

"Yes, where else are you going to stay?"

"Good question."

"Right, so I thought I'd take you home with me."

"But what about my uncle? Shouldn't we go to the authorities?"

"Let's not worry about that right now. One thing at a time. For now, you're sticking with me. When we get to my house, I'll ask my father what to do."

We marched on. Soon we were out of the woods and standing on an old dirt road. Crossing the other side, I spotted an inn.

"That's where we're going?" I said.

"Yes, I live there. My parents run it. Technically, it's a house, but they remodeled it to look like an inn. It's a family-owned business. Come on, there's nothing to worry about." She gestured to me, charging across the gravel road.

When we reached it, I noticed the house was three stories high. In front of it, there was an iron gate. It was open, so guests could enter. Next to it was a sign that read Whimple Inn. Inspecting it, I spotted a family coming out. A couple with four kids walked past us.

"Hey," said Dori, tapping me on the shoulder.

"What?"

"Come on, let's go!"

Shortly after, we entered the house. The first thing I noticed was the oak floors and the hanging chandeliers. *Wow, this is really something!*

"How many rooms are there?" I asked.

"Forty. The first and second floors are where the guests stay," explained Dori. "The top floor is reserved for the family. We have twenty guest rooms. Come on, we need to go see my dad."

We entered the library on the third floor. It was full of all kinds of books. I then noticed two empty chairs in front of a desk. One chair was behind it though. And sitting in it was Dori's father. I could tell he was a tall, slender man. He wore gold spectacles, hanging on a chain. He was using them to read a book.

"Hello, Dori, who's your friend?" asked Mr. Whimple. He didn't even glance up.

"This is Eddie. Eddie…"

"Eddie Razor," I answered. "It's a pleasure to meet you."

Mr. Whimple took off his glasses and stared at me. "Did you say Eddie Razor?"

"Yes, sir."

"I heard your name on the radio!"

"What?"

"I think, you should sit down," he said, gesturing to a chair.

Mr. Whimple explained that my uncle's house caught fire and burned down. They found his charred remains. The police thought I was dead too.

"We have to go to the station and tell them you're alive," said Mr. Whimple, getting up. He then turned his attention to his daughter. "Dori, you stay here!"

3

Mr. Whimple set things straight. But another issue arose. What was going to happen to me? Now that my uncle was dead, would I be sent to a children's home? I sat on a chair in the police station. Earlier I had been bombarded by the newscast, but now I felt lonely. I thought about my uncle, Count Razor. When I was first adopted by him, I didn't know he'd be so evil. I had to move South to live with him.

"My name is Count Razor. And you're here because you have the gift." He shoved me in a room, locking it.

"What the…! Hey, you can't keep me in here!"

"Sorry, but this is your home now."

"But!"

"You'll learn to like me."

But I couldn't. So, when the opportunity came, I fled. But I never imagined he'd die in a house fire…

Suddenly, Dori entered the building with her mother, snapping me to reality.

"Guess what?" she asked, rushing to me. "We're related!"

"Yeah, that's great," I answered. "Wait, what?! What did you say?"

"I said, we're related."

"But how?"

"It turns out you're my second cousin."

"You're kidding!"

"No, it's true," said Mrs. Whimple, stopping in front of me. She was a tall, slender woman with long, brown hair. "Your mother is my first cousin."

"That explains why you're a You-Know-What," replied Dori, giving me a wink.

It was almost too much to take in. I stared at Mrs. Whimple and had a flashback. She was at my family's funeral months back. I just didn't realize who she was, but now I recognized her.

"Then that means you can adopt me," I said, looking at her.

"Well, I'm certainly going to try. Would you like that?"

"Oh yes, please!"

"Then I'm going to do my best to see that it happens."

And she did. But it took a lot of hard work. Mr. and Mrs. Whimple had to get help from an adoption agency. From there, they went through the court system and met its requirements. And "finally" after six months, I was "officially" adopted.

4

Living with the Whimple family was quite a change. I was now one of them which was great but hard to except. After all, this was my second day of "officially" being Eddie Whimple instead of Eddie Razor. And in my mind, it still hadn't clicked.

I stared at my new bedroom on the third floor. A wooden bed sat on a black and white Persian rug. Mrs. Whimple had given me a black comforter to cover the bed. Next to it sat a wooden bedside table with a small tv on top. And in the far corner, there was an antique dresser. There was also a wardrobe. I unpacked my clothes and put stuff in boxes under the bed. Seeing there wasn't much else to do, I left my room and went to the first floor.

"Come on, Eddie!" I felt a tug on my arm.

It was Dori. I hurried after her into the dining room and nearly bumped into one of the round tables in the room. Several guests turned and stared. Mrs. Whimple approached us, speaking.

"Oh, Dori, there you are!"

"Hey, mom! What's the matter?"

"Could you guys do me a big favor?" She glanced over her shoulder at the guests. "It's almost noon, and I need you to go to the store and get supplies for me. Here are the things I need." She handed a list to Dori. "Oh, and here's the money! Be sure to put it in your pocket, so you won't lose it."

"Sure, mom," said Dori, taking it.

"Great! In the meantime, I'll stay here and check on the guests. See you two later!"

We then exited the inn.

5

"What's the name of this place again?" I asked.

"Watalu (Watt-a-loo). You officially live just outside the small town of Watalu."

"Wata what?"

"Watalu." She pointed to a green, rectangular sign in front of us. Its name was written in white letters. "The population is only 93."

"You mean, 94." I smiled. "Don't forget about me."

She rolled her eyes. "Anyway, the only store is about half a mile away," she said, scanning the dirt road. "Any more questions?"

"Yeah, how do other shapeshifters know to stop at the inn?"

"The inn is open to anyone, but there is a special sign to let them know they can stop there."

"What is it?"

"A butterfly weathervane."

"Really?"

"Yep, it represents metamorphosis. It sits on top of the house."

"Cool."

"It's the universal symbol for all shapeshifters."

Dori stopped in her tracks.

"What's the matter?" I asked.

"Nothing, but I thought we could practice using our skills while we're out here."

"You mean, shapeshift?"

"Yes, silly. There's no one around. Well…" She put her hands on her hip.

"Well, the thing is…" I shuffled my feet. "I haven't exactly been practicing. So, I…"

"I thought so." She glared.

"What?"

"You act like using your ability is horrible!"

"It's not that… It's just strange."

"You have a gift! And you need to use it!"

"Okay, so… What do you want me to do?"

"Transform into a cat."

"A cat?! I've never done a cat." I suddenly felt shaky and weak in the knees. "I don't think I can do this…"

"You know what a cat looks like," said Dori. "Right…?"

"Well, yes!"

"So, just visualize it inside your mind. Like this!" And she transformed into a cat. A few seconds later, she changed back. "Now it's your turn!"

Great! Why couldn't she have chosen a wolf instead?

Dori laughed. "Because I want you to transform into a cat."

I then closed my eyes, trying to form an image. When I opened my eyes, I heard laughing. *You got to be kidding me!*

"Looks like you're only half done." She giggled.

My face turned red. But it was true. I was stuck in a half cat/half human state.

"I don't suppose people like hybrids," I mumbled.

"Not this girl. Come on, finish it out!"

I closed my eyes and took a deep breath. When I opened my eyes, I couldn't believe it. I had "actually" done it. Other than being a cat, the only other thing I had successfully transformed into was a wolf.

6

We arrived at the store and bought all the things Mrs. Whimple wanted. Soon we were back at the inn.

"Dorrri!"

We turned to see Edith. She was a tall, blond haired woman with blue eyes.

"Oh hey, Aunt Edith!" greeted Dori.

"Hey, sweetie, I've been looking for you."

"You have?"

"Yes, your mom wants the food you picked up from the store. She sent me to find you."

I almost fell over. I was carrying an armload of groceries.

"Dori, why don't you help him," said Edith. "Your mom's waiting in the dining room. We don't want any accidents."

Dori grabbed a bag, and we hurried away. A moment later, we set the groceries on a table in the dining room. Mrs. Whimple rushed up.

"Oh good, you got everything I needed," she said, scanning the food. "What took you so long?"

I started to answer, but Dori slapped her hand over my mouth. That got Mrs. Whimple's attention.

"What were you going to say?" asked Mrs. Whimple, putting her hands on her hip.

I glance over at Dori and watched her turn her back on me.

"Ahem." Mrs. Whimple waited for me to answer.

"I was going to say that we were practicing."

"Practicing…" She frowned. "Practicing what? Not… metamorphosis."

I nodded my head.

"In broad daylight when you haven't had any proper training?!"

"But mom I've done it hundreds of times!" said Dori, turning back around.

"Dori, how many times have I told you? You have to wait! What if someone saw you?

"There was no one around!"

"It doesn't matter!" Mrs. Whimple then glanced back at some of the guests in the dining room. She lowered her voice. "I'm so mad at you right now, I could spit. You're lucky I have guests to attend to! We'll discuss this later… In the meantime, I want you and Eddie to go upstairs and meet your new teacher."

"Teacher!" said Dori, nearly falling over.

"Yes, he just arrived today. Go see your uncle at the front desk. He'll tell you which room he's in."

Dori stomped off.

"Dori, slow down!" I said, trying to keep up.

"You had to open your mouth!"

"Dori, wait! You're blaming this all on me," I said, grabbing her shoulder. "You didn't even tell me we're not supposed to do it."

Dori stopped in her tracks. "No, you're right. It's just…" She sighed. "It's just ever since I found out I had the ability a year ago, I've been so excited, wanting to learn more. And I just feel like my mom is holding me back."

"Why?"

"I guess, it's because she and dad got to go to the academy growing up."

"Academy?"

"Yes, it's the only one in the world for shapeshifters. It's a private school far away. They allow students to join at eleven years old if they have the gift."

"Wow, that sounds amazing."

"Yeah, if I were going… Instead I'm stuck here!" She clinched her fists.

"Have you always been homeschooled?"

"Yes, my whole life. My dad usually helps me with my studies. But this year is different… What about you?"

"No, I went to a normal public school before…" My heart sank. "Before my parents and brothers died."

"What was it like?"

"Eh, it's school," I said, trying to hide my sadness. "I… I always hated riding the bus. The school work wasn't too bad. Mostly I just miss my friends…"

Dori perked up. "Friends?"

"Well, that was a long time ago. I haven't heard from them, since I ended up in the children's home. Not that I didn't try to make friends there, but it just wasn't the same. I guess, it was because I knew I was going to bc adopted."

I suddenly felt sad again. I hadn't thought about my friends in a long time. *They probably don't even remember me...*

"Hey," said Dori, putting her hand on my shoulder. "I'm sorry."

I didn't want sympathy though... But I felt hurt. Mostly because I realized how much I missed my family. It had been over a year, since they died. And all the changes I had gone through didn't make things any easier. But I didn't want Dori to know.

"Come on," I said, changing the subject. "Let's go meet our new teacher."

7

We stopped at the front desk to see Dori's uncle. He was a lanky man, who had short, brown hair and blue eyes. He was Mrs. Whimple's older brother. When he noticed us, he smiled.

"Hi, Uncle Oliver," said Dori. "We're here to…"

"Don't say another word," he interrupted. "I know exactly why you're here."

"You do?" I said.

"Yep, your teacher is in room 309."

"Thanks," answered Dori.

"Don't mention it." He winked.

We hurried to the top floor. Dori kept frowning.

"What's the matter?" I asked.

"The teacher is staying on the third floor."

"So?"

"So, the third floor has always been reserved for the family."

"I guess, your parents made an exception."

"Yeah, I guess… It's strange."

When we reached the room, we knocked on the front door.

"Yes, who is it?"

"It's me, Dori. I'm Edith's daughter, and this is…"

The door swung open. An old, chubby man peered at us from behind square, framed glasses. He wore a nice dress shirt with a tie and black dress pants.

"I take it you're my students."

"Yes," I answered.

"Come with me."

He walked out of his room, closing the door behind him. We followed him down the hallway to room 310.

"Your father fixed this room for us," he said, pulling out a key.

He unlocked the door and entered, turning on the light switch. I stared in shock when I realized the room was set up like a classroom. There were two student chair desks, a black office desk, and one office chair. There was even a large, green, chalk board, hanging on the wall. I guess, they didn't have a smart board.

"I suppose, you know why your parents hired me to be your teacher," he said, sitting on the office chair."

"No, not really," said Dori, sitting on a student chair desk. "We only found out about you today."

He raised an eyebrow.

"Dori's used to being homeschooled," I explained, sitting down on the other student chair desk.

"Ah, I see." He rubbed his nose. "So, are you siblings?"

"Cousins," I answered. "I was just recently adopted."

His eyebrows furrowed, digesting this information. He then cleared his throat. "Have either of you ever heard of the Academy of Gifted Teknon (Tek'-non). Also known as AGT School."

Dori's eyebrows shot up.

"Ah, I see one of you has." He smiled.

"You're from there?" she questioned. "The school for shapeshifters."

"Yes, I taught there."

"What are you doing here?" I asked.

"I'm part of a special program that allows me to teach students who can't personally attend the academy. It was the school board's idea. Since there is only one school for shapeshifters, and not everybody can attend. The school offers the program to parents who want their child or children to be taught properly. In addition, the school promises scholarship funds to every student who participates and passes this one-year program."

"Wow," said Dori. "How come I've never heard of it."

"Well, the program has only been around for five years. Anyway, my job is to teach you how to hone your skills properly."

"Sweet," answered Dori.

"I will also be helping you with your regular schoolwork as well."

I let out a groan.

"Sorry, but it can't be all fun and games. So, let's start with introductions. I'm James Needle. And you are…," he gestured to us.

"Dori Whimple, and this is Eddie."

"Nice to meet you both, and how old are you?"

"I'm thirteen," answered Dori.

"I will turn thirteen soon, sir," I said.

"Really?"

"Yes, my birthday is May 16th."

"I see. Well, I look forward to celebrating your birthday in a few days." He wiggled his eyebrows. "So." He clasped his hands together. "When did you guys first notice your ability?"

"About…. eight months ago," answered Dori.

"Basically, the same," I replied.

"And what was the first animal you turned into?" he asked Dori.

"A cat."

"And you?"

"A wolf."

"A wolf? Hm… now that is interesting."

"Why?" I asked, suddenly nervous.

"Well, it's just unusual that's all. For most students, it's either a cat or a dog."

"Oh, well… when my parents were alive, we used to have a wolf."

"Really?"

"Yeah, my dad found a wolf cub, and we… My brothers and I helped raised it. But then mom insisted we release it back into the wild."

"I see. So." He said, rubbing his fingers. "Do you guys understand why you are shapeshifters?"

"It's in our genes," answered Dori.

"Right, it's passed from parent to child. Usually the gift is triggered by changes of adolescence, transitioning into adulthood."

"Say that again?" I asked.

"When you start developing into an adult," he answered.

"Oh."

"A shapeshifter's cells allow them to take on different forms. But there are limitations."

"I still don't see how that's possible," I answered.

"In what way?" asked Mr. Needle.

"Well, how can I do something when I don't understand or… realize that I'm doing it?"

"Yeah, I don't understand either," confessed Dori.

"Well," he said, rubbing his nose. "Both of you breathe air, right?"

"Yeah, so," said Dori.

"So, you don't tell your heart to pump and lungs to work when you're sleeping. Do you? Think of your gift in the same way. When you shapeshift and visualize the animal you want to transform into, your brain gives directions without you realizing it."

"Whoa," I said. "I never realized that before."

"Right. But moving on. Let's start with what you're familiar with. So!" He said, standing up. "You both have successfully transformed into at least one animal."

We both nodded.

"Tell me, what is the difference between you when you transform into an animal verses a real animal?" he asked, leaning against the office desk.

"Well, I'm a human," said Dori.

"Right, what else?"

"Well, as a human I um… I don't think like an animal when I transform into one."

"Right, what else?"

"Well…"

Dori and I shrugged our shoulders.

"I'm guessing both of you have transformed with your clothes on. Right? Don't you think that's strange?"

"That never occurred to me," said Dori.

"Because your clothes get blended into the metamorphosis process. If you don't wear the right clothes, you'll look pretty strange when you transform into an animal."

Dori blushed.

"I'm guessing you didn't realize that because you can't see yourself when you transform. If you wear bright pink, then you might turn into a pink cat. A shapeshifter has to be very careful about wearing the right clothing when using metamorphosis, or they'll stand out. Usually black or white clothing is your safe bet when transforming into a cat... And since you transform with your clothes on, it's not like you're actually becoming an animal. It's more like an outer covering to create an illusion. A trained shapeshifter can tell the difference between a real animal, and a person who's disguising them self." Mr. Needle then noticed Dori's odd expression. "Is something bothering you?"

"It's just that... I can only transform into a cat or a dog. When I try other animals like a bird, it doesn't work. Why is that?"

"Because your gift has limitations. A shapeshifter can only transform into mammals that are of the Canidae and Felidae family. So, this!" He said, pulling out a piece of paper from his pocket. "Will be your first assignment."

"Assignment?" I answered.

"Yes, this is a list of every Canidae and Felidae animal that a shapeshifter has ever transformed into. I want you to memorize this list. And it wouldn't hurt to look up each animal as well. Do you have a computer to use?"

"I have a laptop," answered Dori.

"Good, you two can share. At the end of the week, I'm going to quiz you to see what you've learned. And now it's time for English. Here are your texts books." He grabbed a couple of English books off the desk. He handed them out and explained that every day from Monday through Friday we would work on a different subject. Saturday was reserved for shapeshifting exercises. Class would start at eight in the morning and end around noon.

8

After our English lesson, we ate some lunch and then went to the library. Dori got out her laptop, and we both sat down on a chair in front of a table.

"Where's the list?" I asked.

"Right here!" She said, holding it up. "The members of the Canidae family include jackals, wolves, dogs, and foxes."

"And the Felidae family?"

"Any of the cat species."

"I've never even heard of some of these. A back-blacked Jackal? Serval?"

"You know, we can probably research these through my dad's books," she said, gesturing to the large shelf beside us. "Look! He has volumes."

"Yep," answered Mr. Whimple, entering the room. "I have tons of books on the Canidae and Felidae."

"Dad, why didn't you tell me?" asked Dori, whirling around.

"Tell you what," he said, peering at her.

"That shapeshifters can't turn into just any animal."

He chuckled. "Would you have believed me?" He then left the room after snatching a book off the shelf.

"Honestly," said Dori. "It's like he doesn't trust me."

"Well, you can't really blame him," I said.

She glared and punched me in the shoulder.

"Ouch!"

"Come on, we've got work to do!"

9

After we did our homework, we decided to go to the lounge on the first floor. We sat on a couch across a coffee table. A game of checkers was set up.

"Want to play?" asked Dori.

"Okay, but I get to be black."

"Fine, but I warn you, I was trained by the best." She cracked her knuckles.

"Of course, you were trained by the best!" said a voice.

I glanced to see a tall man with a turned-up mustache.

"Hi, grandpa, have you come to watch the game?" asked Dori.

"I'd like to, but I'm afraid, I'm on business right now. Perhaps I'll watch later, if you guys are still playing."

"Okay, see you later!"

And he left the room.

"So, Dori," I said, moving a checker piece. "I know Oliver is your mom's brother."

"Yep, her only brother."

"Right, but what about your dad? Does he have any siblings?"

"Three brothers, and they all live up North."

"Really?"

"Yep, my dad's not originally from here. He moved South to marry my mom. Grandma and Grandpa thought they needed help running the inn, so they moved here too."

"Do your uncles ever come to see you?"

"Winter makes it hard for travel. I usually get Christmas cards from them in the mail. We probably won't see them until summer. Usually we close the inn down for two weeks in June to visit."

"Are they married?"

"Yep. But no worries. You'll get a chance to meet the entire family later."

"Okay, Dori, but there's just one problem."

"What?"

"It's your move!"

She stuck her tongue out at me.

"Hey!"

She then captured three of my checker pieces. My jaw dropped.

"Told you I was good," she smirked. "It's your turn!"

But she knew I was beat. No matter what. My pieces were going to get jumped, and so I let her jump them.

"Yes, I won! I beat you!"

"Come on, Dori, give me a break!"

"Haaa! Ha! Ha! Ha!" She stood up and did a happy dance.

"And stop bragging!"

"Sorry, do you want to play again?"

"No, I want to do something else."

And we left the lounge.

10

The following morning, we met with our teacher to work on our school lesson. Today was History.

"Eddie, would you recite the lesson?" asked Mr. Needle.

I suddenly felt anxious. I loved History, but I hated being put on the spot. Shortly after, I felt a tingling sensation and was on all fours. Dori's mouth dropped open, and I lowered my head in embarrassment. I accidentally transformed into a wolf. *Why did that happen?*

"It's your hormones, Eddie," said Mr. Needle. "I've had a few embarrassing moments in my youth as well. As you get older, you'll be more in control of your ability. Has this been happening a lot?"

Just every now and then. I was always lucky that nobody saw me at the children's home.

"I might need to work with you on breathing exercises to calm your anxiety," said Mr. Needle. "Do you think you can transform back?"

I nodded. A few seconds later, I was back to my normal self. I then noticed my shoes were on the floor and put them on.

"Eddie," said Mr. Needle. "I don't mean to pry. But how long were you in the children's home?"

"Originally, I was there around six months, or so before my uncle adopted me."

"Uncle?"

"That was the first time. He knew I was different and was going to raise me like him, but he... He was evil. After he died in the house fire, I ended up in the home again for another six months, until the Whimple family adopted me."

"How did your family die?"

"Car accident."

"I see. This... has been a rough year for you."

All at once I felt emotional but didn't want to admit it. I frowned not wanting to think about it. Mr. Needle sensed this, and we went back to the History lesson.

When I got out of class, I realized it was raining outside. I was disappointed, because I wanted to go out.

I then entered the dining room and made a sandwich. I sat down at a round table. Dori quickly joined me.

"We can still go outside," said Dori, munching on her food. "Or… we can play checkers."

"No, not checkers!" I said, groaning.

"Why not, after all… I was trained by the best," she grinned, cracking her knuckles.

"That's why I don't want to play against you!"

"Why don't you guys help in the kitchen?" We turned to see Mr. Whimple.

"No, I think, I'll pass this time," said Dori.

"I'm sure, your mother would appreciate it," he said, peering at her.

"Oh alright."

"Good, and you can help too, Eddie."

We cleaned up after ourselves and scurried into the kitchen.

"Oh good, you've come to clean!" said Mrs. Whimple. She almost bumped into us. "Edith and Oliver are washing dishes."

They quickly waved at us, turning back to their work. Grandma Whimple was also in the kitchen. She had just walked in, carrying a broom and a dust pan.

"Thanks!" said Mrs. Whimple, snatching the items.

"No problem. Is there anything else I can do for you, sweetie?"

"No, not unless you want to check the tables again to make sure everything's clean."

"Okay, sounds good to me," said Grandma Whimple, leaving the kitchen.

"Here, Eddie, you can sweep the floor," said Mrs. Whimple, handing me the broom and dustpan. "Dori, you can help your aunt and uncle dry the dishes." She handed her a dishtowel.

"I'm going to see if anything else needs to be done." And she exited the kitchen.

11

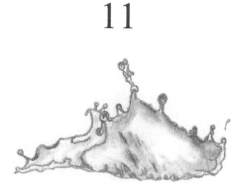

When we left the kitchen, we were shocked to find water pouring across the floor.

"What's going on?" I asked.

"I don't know!" answered Dori. "But let's find out!"

The entire first floor was flooded with two inches of water.

"What a mess!" said Dori.

It was also crowded. People were everywhere. Finally, we figured out what happened. The local water tower nearby had a large hole in it. Someone had repeatedly shot at it with a gun. Because of the hole, water gushed out, causing the water level to drop. And because it was raining, the entire surrounding area became flooded, causing more damage. Within the next few hours, every single guest left the inn, except Mr. Needle.

"Wow, the inn seems so empty," said Dori.

We wandered around the second floor. Mr. and Mrs. Whimple told us to stay upstairs. Some people were supposed to come by and help fix the damage. Dori's uncle then collided into us.

"There you are!" said Oliver. "Your parents wanted me to tell you that they're going to the store. Edith and I are going with them."

"Where's grandma and grandpa?" asked Dori.

"Minding the front desk to let visitors know we're closed. I'll see you later!" He hurried away.

"I wish we could go outside," I said.

"Who says we can't?" answered Dori.

"You're parents."

She cocked her eyes.

"And what about our clothes?" I asked. "We'll get them soaking wet."

"They're already soaking wet!"

"I don't know…"

"Come on!" And Dori grabbed my arm.

A moment later, we were down the stairs and out the front door, sloshing through water.

"We're going to get in so much trouble for this," I said, splashing around.

"Who cares?" answered Dori, shoving me.

But we stopped when we noticed a tall man approach, his dark shadow overcasting us.

"Sorry, but you're coming with me," he said, pulling out a gun.

Our eyes went wide.

"Let's not make a scene. I know what you two are."

"What do you mean?" I asked.

"Move it, shapeshifters! Your father has something I want."

"I don't understand," said Dori, turning pale in the face.

"Just do as I say, and nobody gets hurt. Now, where's your father's study?"

12

The man held a gun to our backs as we entered the house. Dori's grandpa was waiting at the front desk. Grandma Whimple was nowhere to be seen.

"I'm sorry, sir," said Grandpa Whimple. "But the inn's closed due to recent damage."

"Well, I work for the DFA, Disaster Flood Areas. My name is Luth McDack. I've come to see the damage."

"Oh, I see. Mr. McDack, will you please wait here?"

Grandpa Whimple left the room, but McDack didn't wait around. He ushered us up the stairs.

"Hurry!" he said, gritting his teeth.

In a matter of seconds, we were shoved up the stairs to the third floor.

"Which room is the study?" asked McDack.

"Room 312," answered Dori.

He pushed us to the locked door. Pulling out a lock pick, he used it to unlock the door. He then attached a firearm muffler to the end of his gun and forced his way in.

"Now stand over there behind the desk," he said, pointing his gun.

"Please, sir," said Dori. Tears were streaming down her cheeks.

"Just do it," I whispered. I was scared too, but I didn't want her to know.

We hurried behind the desk as he started searching through Mr. Whimple's papers. He opened drawers, searching through files. A smile then formed on his face when he noticed the laptop inside the desk drawer. However, his smile faded when he heard a low grow. He turned to see a black panther, charging at him. With one swipe of the cat's paw, his gun went crashing to the ground. With another swipe, he was knocked unconscious.

We watched in amazement as the cat transformed into a human.

"Mr. Needle?" said Dori.

"Are you two alright?" He asked, straightening himself.

We nodded.

"Good. Do you have a cellphone on you?"

"Yes, I've got one," said Dori, handing it to him.

"Don't you have one?" I asked.

"I never carry one with me when I transform. Even if I did, it would just fall to the ground. Electronic devices don't blend into metamorphosis like your clothes do. And... neither do my glasses or some of my shoes. I can't see the numbers on this cellphone. Would one of you please retrieve my glasses for me from my room. They should be on my dresser."

I dashed away. A moment later, I returned with his glasses.

"Thank you!" he said, taking them.

"Who are you calling?" asked Dori.

"Someone who will take care of this man. If you don't mind, I'd like the two of you to step out into the hall."

13

After he was done talking on the phone, he called us back into the room.

"Mr. Needle, what's going on?" asked Dori. "Who is this man? He said his name is Luth McDack."

"I can't personally tell you who this man is," he said. "But what I can tell you is this. He's the one who repeatedly shot at the water tower, until there was a hole. It was just enough to create a diversion to get inside the inn."

"Why?" asked Dori.

"Because your father works for a top-secret organization. And this man was looking for a list, a list of every shapeshifter on record.

"You mean, so that he could…" And I did the kill sign.

"Precisely. Anyway, here's your cellphone back, Dori." He gave it to her. "And don't bother looking up the number on your phone. I've deleted it off."

Shortly after, the rest of the Whimple family rushed into the room. When Grandpa Whimple realized that Luth McDack was a fraud, he informed the rest of the family.

"Are the children alright?" asked Mrs. Whimple. She noticed us.

"Everything's been taken care of," said Mr. Needle. "There will be some men coming by to take care of this... man." He said, gesturing to Luth McDack on the floor.

"Dori," said Mrs. Whimple. "Why don't you and Eddie go watch a movie."

We glanced at each other. We understood the adults didn't want us around. So, we left. About thirty minutes later, some people did come by.

14

The next day it was reported that a man had been arrested for blowing up the water tower. It was the same person, Luth McDack.

"You mean, they've caught the man," said Grandpa Whimple, winking.

"Yes, sweetie, that's what it says in the newspaper," answered Grandma Whimple, smiling.

Of course, we all knew what happened.

Dori and I ate breakfast and then hurried to our classroom. It was time for school, and soon we were seated at our desks, waiting patiently. We grinned when Mr. Needle entered the room. He eyed us from behind his glasses.

"I suppose, you want to know more about what happened yesterday," he said.

"I just wanted to say that you were AMAZING yesterday," replied Dori.

"If you're referring to a very fat panther, then I'll have to agree with you," answered Mr. Needle. "I really should go on a diet. But in all seriousness don't ever do what I did yesterday, until you're properly trained. I could have been killed."

"So, when do we get to practice morphing into a panther?" asked Dori.

"Not for a good while, young lady. And now… it's time for Math!"

Dori wrinkled her nose.

"Come on, it's not that bad," I said.

"Speak for yourself," answered Dori.

Mr. Needle chuckled. Grabbing a piece of chalk, he started writing problems on the board.

"Today, we're going to be working on fractions!"

15

After class was over, I discovered a lemon meringue pie in the dining room. The entire family was waiting for me. They already had the candles stuck in it.

"You didn't think we'd forget your birthday," said Mrs. Whimple. "Did you?" She placed the pie on a table in front of me. And lit the candles with strike on matches.

"Well, I…"

"The house may be a wreck," replied Grandpa Whimple. "But we saved the dessert."

"Or at least my sister did," said Oliver, winking.

"We also got you some presents," replied Grandma Whimple, setting them on the table.

"Go ahead," said Mr. Whimple. "Sit down, and we'll sing to you."

I sat in a chair, and Edith pulled out a camera, taking pictures of me. The whole family then sang "Happy Birthday." Even Mr. Needle joined in.

Afterwards, I opened my presents from everyone. They bought me things that I might need. I got clothes, a blanket, and shoes.

When I was done opening my gifts, the entire family, except for Dori, went back to fixing the flood damage from yesterday. On a good note, the water tower's hole had been patched. So, things were on the mend. Dori and I ate our lunches quickly.

"Why don't you two go outside and play for a while," said Mrs. Whimple, cleaning up. "You can help later."

16

It was a cloudy, summer day, and I could tell there was a change in the weather. The warm wind blew against the house. Dori walked off the front porch and stood beside me. She had something in her hand.

"What's that?" I asked.

"Oh, it's my watch." She showed it to me. It was a silver pocket watch. "My dad bought it from a collector and gave it to me. It's really old. You have to use a key to wind it."

"That's so cool! May I see it?"

"Sure." She handed it to me.

I took the watch and examined it. After a moment, I gave it back to her, and she placed it in her pocket.

"Well, what shall we do?" I asked.

"Well, I can't transform, or I'll lose my watch."

"Huh. Oh yeah, I forgot that you can't transform with certain objects."

"That's right. It depends on what it is. Most clothing can blend into the metamorphosis process, if there isn't too much metal on it, like buttons."

"What happens if there's too much metal."

"I guess, they pop off. I've noticed several of my clothes are missing buttons."

Dori scanned the area. She reminded me of a pirate, looking out over the waves. It was as if she were searching for treasure. The wind blew her hair around.

"Most of the water has receded from the day before," she reported. "And I can see the new patch on the water tower where that man shot a hole in it."

"I'm glad they fixed it," I answered. "When do you think the inn will be open to the public?"

"Mom says that everything should be ready by next Monday. It's been kind of strange with no guests around. Come on, let's go for a walk!"

17

On Thursday most of the damage on the first floor was finally fixed. It took a lot of hard work, but things paid off. Dori and I quickly ate breakfast and were ready for another lecture day with Mr. Needle.

"Guess what we're learning today?" asked Mr. Needle, leaning against the office desk.

"I don't know," said Dori. "What?"

"Animal science! I thought it would be a great idea if we started studying the biology of the Canidae and Felidae to help you gain a better understanding. And..." He held up his hand. "I understand that you've been studying the list I gave you on Monday."

Dori grinned, but I turned pale.

"No worries. Your quiz isn't until Saturday. However, if you remember back on Monday, I encouraged you to look up the animals on the list."

We nodded.

"So, today we will be looking at the strengths and weakness of some of these animals. By studying their biology, it will help you in the future. I've printed off a worksheet for each of you. It has facts covering the strengths and weaknesses of Canidae and Felidae animals." He then gave us the handouts. "Silently read over the worksheet first. When you're both done, we'll go over it."

18

After class was over, we headed out of the room. In doing so, Mr. Needle stopped me.

"Oh, Eddie, I almost forgot."

"Yes, sir."

"If you still want to, after lunch I can teach you those breathing exercises to help you with your anxiety."

"Oh. Yeah, sure. I'd like that."

"Good, then I'll see you back here at two."

"Sure." I then rushed down the hall after Dori.

"What did he want?" she asked, waiting patiently.

"To teach me some breathing exercises. I'm supposed to meet him back in the classroom at two."

"Oh, will you be alright?"

"Sure, why wouldn't I be?"

"No reason."

"Come on! Let's go eat lunch, I'm starving!"

A minute later, we were in the dining room, fixing ourselves a plate of homecooked food. *Sweet!* I could never get enough of this kind of food. While eating, Dori and I goofed off, until it was time for me to meet with Mr. Needle. I then waved goodbye to her.

"See you later, Dori!"

"See you, Eddie! Remember it's a breathing exercise! So, don't hold your breath!"

"Ha, ha! Very funny!" I turned, almost running into Mr. Whimple. "Oops, sorry, sir."

He raised his eyebrows, and I passed on by.

19

Just Breathe!

I entered the classroom to find Mr. Needle already there. He was sitting in the office chair, wheeling around. He stopped when he noticed me.

"Oh good. Are you ready to begin?"

I nodded, but I felt tense. Without Dori around, it felt strange.

"Relax. I only bite when I'm a panther." I cracked a smile.

"See! Good for the face muscles. Now take a deep breath."

Mr. Needle then went over the fundamentals of some breathing exercises. And we practiced them together. I felt silly doing them, but I went along with it. After about forty minutes, I finally felt comfortable.

"See, you're doing just fine," said Mr. Needle.

But then I deflated.

"A, ah. None of that." He waggled his finger.

I then broke into laughter. I couldn't help it.

"Someone's got the simples. Take a deep breath."

But it only made it worse. After a moment, I finally calmed down.

"Okay, I'm good now," I said.

"Are you sure?" he asked, raising his eyebrows.

"Yeah, I think so." Something then occurred to me, and I stopped smiling.

"What's the matter, Eddie?"

"Nothing, I was just thinking."

"About what?" He leaned forward.

"Well, I was just thinking. What... made you decide to do the program to... come here?"

"You mean, besides the fact that it was the school board's idea?"

"Yeah."

"I realized there was potential not being recognized. I was one of the first teachers to teach at the academy."

"How long has the academy been around?"

"52 years."

"How old are you again?"

"76."

"Shouldn't you be retired or something."

"Eddie Whimple! I'm surprised at you."

"Sorry, it's just… Well, I knew you were old. But…"

"One day you'll get there too." He said, peering at me behind his glasses. "Or I'll at least make sure that you do." He wiggled his eyebrows. "Anyway, since I was getting… Ahem!" He pretended to clear his throat. "Old. I decided to try something different, a new challenge so to speak. And it has been a new learning experience for me."

"It has?"

"Yes, teaching is always a learning experience in my book. So, is there anything else you need help with?"

"Nope, I think, I'm good."

"Good. Then your breathing exercise is over for today. I expect you back in this classroom around eight in the morning."

20

I left the classroom, searching for Dori but couldn't find her. I bumped into Grampa Whimple.

"Watch it there!" he said, stepping to the side. "Are you looking for Dori?"

"Yes, have you seen her?"

"I think, she's in the kitchen."

"Thanks!" I took off, running. I almost bumped into Dori's aunt.

"Eddie!" said Edith. "You know there's no running in the inn. Walk. Don't run. We don't want any accidents."

Carefully, I hurried down the stairs, until I reached the first floor. I spotted Dori in a heartbeat. She noticed me and walked over.

"So, how did it go?" asked Dori.

"It was alright."

"Did you learn to breathe properly," she teased.

"Yes." I stuck out my tongue. "Come on! Let's go outside."

"I can't. Mom wants me to vacuum the lounge rooms."

"Oh."

"Here, Eddie," said Mr. Whimple, strolling by. "You might want this." He handed me a feather duster. "I have orders to put you on maid duty."

"Thanks…"

"Go on. Hop to it!" He ushered.

"Come on," said Dori. "I'll show you the rounds."

She took me all around the first floor, showing me where I needed to dust.

"You have to dust all the chairs, tables, TVs, lamps, etc.… I'll get the vacuum cleaner!"

And she did while I dusted. Oliver stopped by and even gave me an apron to wear.

"Nice one, Uncle Oliver!" said Dori, giving him two thumbs up.

"Just you wait, Dori," I remarked. "Your turn is coming."

Oliver rushed off, laughing. Grandma Whimple then stopped by.

"My don't you make a lovely maid," she said.

"Uh… thanks. Oliver gave it to me."

She winked at me and hurried away. Dori then turned on the vacuum cleaner and started vacuuming.

21

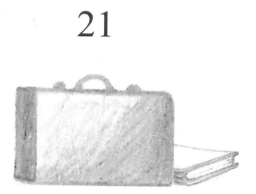

I entered the classroom at eight on Friday. Dori beat me to the room. We had a race, and she won.

"Ha, ha!" She said and did her happy dance.

"It would've been a different story, if I hadn't tripped in the hall," I muttered.

Mr. Needle then walked into the room, carrying an art case and book.

"Did I hear little footsteps running down the hall," he said.

I suddenly froze. "Breathe" he mouthed to me. And I started smiling.

"Next time, walk," he replied, trying to be serious. "Today we're going to do Art."

"Yes!" said Dori, sitting down at her desk.

"I want you guys to draw pictures that express yourself."

"That sounds like fun!" replied Dori.

"It would be if I could draw," I said, grumbling.

"They don't have to be perfect," answered Mr. Needle. "You can draw anything you want as long as it's appropriate. You have ten minutes to work on them. I'll even do some myself. And when time's up, we'll talk about our drawings and what they mean." Mr. Needle set his things down on the office desk and handed out notebook papers and utensils.

Taking a pencil, I started working on my drawing. I drew a wolf, well sort of… It looked more like a circle with stick legs. Then I decided to draw a baseball. At least that would be easy to draw. *But what else?* I liked school, so I decided to draw Mr. Needle as a stick figure. I was done before ten minutes, but Dori was still scribbling away. Finally, time was up.

"Okay, does everybody have their drawings ready?" asked Mr. Needle.

"I'm done," answered Dori.

"Me too," I replied.

"Good. In that case, I'll go first." He held up his drawing. "These are some illustrations that express me. This…" He gestured. "Is a book. It may not look like one, but that's what it is. Because I love to read. And this…" He pointed with his finger. "Is a teacher. Because I'm a teacher, and I love to teach. See!" He moved his finger across the paper. "The teacher's smiling. And this…" He motioned. "If you can believe it or not. Is a fat panther."

I smiled. It looked just as bad as my wolf drawing.

"Anyway, it represents my metamorphosis, and I thought it would humor you. Okay, so who's next?"

"Me!" said Dori, and she held up her paper for us to see. Unlike me, she actually had artistic talent. She pointed to a cat. "This represents me. Because I love cats! And these…" She gestured. "Are music notes! Because I love music!"

"Is there anything you don't like?" I asked.

She stuck her tongue out at me. Mr. Needle laughed.

"And this is a TV! Because I love…"

"Movies!" I finished.

"Yes!"

"And who's that?" I asked, pointing to an elaborate stick person.

"That's you, cuz!"

"Oh."

"Yep, because we're friends."

"Aww!" said Mr. Needle.

"Your turn!" She grinned.

"Well," I said. "I'm not that great of a drawer, but I'll do my best to explain." I held up my artwork. "This is a wolf." I pointed. "I feel like it represents me, because sometimes I feel like a loner."

Dori stopped smiling.

"I guess, it's because of how much change I've gone through this year. And because it also represents my metamorphosis." I cleared my throat. "And this…" I gestured. "Is a baseball. I used to love playing catch with my friends at my old school."

"Is this me?" asked Dori, pointing to my stick drawing.

"No, that's Mr. Needle."

"Oh, I see. He's got a big belly."

Mr. Needle frowned.

"I drew you, Mr. Needle, because I like school."

"How come you didn't draw me?" asked Dori.

"Because you're too pretty," I said, sticking out my tongue.

"Hmph!"

Mr. Needle laughed. "Well, I'm glad we all got to express each other with our art. Now it's time for us to look at other artists who express themselves in different ways. So, I brought a book that tells us about their works." He took the book off his desk and began to read out loud.

22

"Hey, Dori! Wait up!" I said, jogging behind her. I had just eaten lunch and was hurrying to catch up. "Where are you going?"

"To grab a ball."

"You have a baseball?"

"No, a tennis ball. But I thought we could play catch with it." She hurried down the hallway.

A few minutes later, she came back with it. And soon we were outside, tossing it back and forth.

"You have a pretty good arm," I said.

"Thanks," she answered. The wind was blowing her hair around.

"So, what made you decide to play catch today?" I asked.

"Well, until today, I didn't even know that you liked baseball," she answered. "Did you used to play a lot with your friends?"

"Yeah and kickball. What about you?"

"No, I usually just throw against the wall." She pointed to the side of the inn.

I examined the house for a moment, admiring its architecture. I remember the first time I saw it, I couldn't believe that it was Dori's home.

"Have you always lived here?" I asked.

"Yes, it's been in my mom's family for generations."

"Really?"

"Yep, you would never know it though, since it's been remodeled so much."

"That is so cool!"

"Eddie!"

The ball hit me in the forehead, and I fell backwards. Dori rushed to me.

"Are you alright?" she asked, peering down at me.

"Yes, it's only a tennis ball." I got up, brushing dirt off my clothes. "I'm pretty klutzy."

"I've noticed." She stuck her tongue out at me. "Race you!" And she took off, running.

23

We played outside, until it was supper time. And, for once, the entire Whimple family, including Mr. Needle, sat down to eat together in the dining room. According to Dori, this was rare. Because the family was usually attending guests at the inn. But since the inn was still closed, it gave everybody an opportunity to eat together for a change. Mr. Whimple ordered pizza for everyone. He thought the ladies needed a break from cooking.

"Yes, I love fresh pizza!" said Dori, taking a bite.

"You're not the only one," I replied. "There's nothing like fresh, cooked pizza."

"Nothing?" said Mr. Needle, wiggling his eyebrows.

I rolled my eyes.

"Say that a little louder," said Dori. "So, my mom can hear."

Mrs. Whimple flashed her eyes at us.

"No way!" I answered. "I'm in enough trouble already."

Grandma and Grandpa Whimple overhead and started laughing.

"Let me be the judge of that, sweetie," said Grandma Whimple.

"I'll second that," replied Grandpa Whimple.

They laughed and went back to eating their pizza.

After everyone had their fill, we decided to visit and play charades. Edith and Oliver stole the limelight. They were good at acting words out. When it was my turn, I gave it my best shot, and Dori made fun of me. But we all still had a great time, and soon it was time for bed.

24

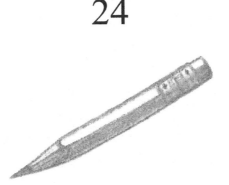

I woke up to a warm, windy Saturday. I could hear the wind howling against the side of the house. I rolled out of bed and got dressed. In a little while, I was downstairs eating eggs and bacon with a glass of cold milk. Dori had already eaten breakfast. She sat next to me at the table, looking over a sheet of paper.

"What are you doing?" I asked.

"Studying. Remember, we've got our quiz today."

"Oh yeah, I forgot." I leaned over and examined the paper. I read over the names of the Canidae and Felidae animals we were supposed to have memorized. I still had thirty minutes before class, but it went by in a breeze. Before I knew it, it was almost eight o-clock.

Dori and I hurried into the classroom and sat down. She took one last look at her paper before Mr. Needle entered the room.

"Guess what time it is?" asked Mr. Needle, setting his things down on the office desk.

"Quiz time!" answered Dori.

"That's right!" He said. "It's quiz time!" He handed each of us a quiz paper and pencil.

I gritted my teeth.

"No cheating!" He waggled his finger. He had us scoot our desks away from each other.

Great! I glanced down at my quiz paper. And I did my best to write all the Canidae and Felidae animals that I was supposed to have memorized. There were also questions typed up that we had to write short answers to.

While we did our quiz, Mr. Needle sat and read a book to pass the time. I'm sure, he was listening to our thoughts though. Every now and then he would peek at us to make sure we weren't cheating. And soon time was up. Mr. Needle snatched our papers and began to read over them. He arched his eyebrows as he studied our papers.

"I can see that one of you didn't study very well," he said, shifting his glasses.

I shrank to the floor. I knew he had to be talking about me.

"I'm not going to mention who it is," he replied. "But I expect you to work hard in the future." He shuffled our papers and put them face down on his desk. "Now, today. We will be starting our very first shapeshifting lesson." He paced the floor. "Dori, would you like to demonstrate?"

"You mean, you want me to transform?" asked Dori.

"That's right."

"Um, okay."

Dori stood up, anxiously.

I'm glad it's not me.

"Eddie," said Mr. Needle. "You're next after her."

I shrank to the floor again. Dori then closed her eyes and transform into a cat.

"Very good," said Mr. Needle. "You actually look like a normal cat. I can see that you've been wearing dark clothes to blend into the metamorphosis better. Now let's see how well you can pretend to be a cat. Remember, you're not a cat. Metamorphosis is only a disguise to give you the appearance of one."

What is it that you want me to do?
Thought Dori.

"Let's see how well you can jump from the floor to your desk."

You want me to jump onto my desk?
"Yes."

Dori turned her head up, examining the distance. *Okay, I'll give it my best shot...* She leaped into the air, hit the side of the desk, and fell. I tried not to laugh. She glared her cat eyes at me.

"What? I didn't say anything!"

"Dori," said Mr. Needle. "Look at me."
She turned her head.

"Remember to use all your senses. Learn to focus your eyes. They will help you to judge the distance to land properly. Try again."

Dori sat on her hunches, stared up, and prepared herself for another leap. This time she was successful. The desk wobbled under her weight.

"Good, now jump down."

Dori leaned her head over the edge of the desk and stared down. *I don't think I can do this...*

"Of course, you can," replied Mr. Needle. "If you can jump up there, you can jump down. Remember, use your eyes to focus. Your inner ear helps with your balance to land properly. You can do it."

Dori jumped down, landing on her feet.

"Thank you, Dori. Now you can turn back. Eddie, it's your turn."

"Do I have to turn into a cat?" I asked, sinking into my chair.

"You can transform into a wolf."

"Okay." And I took a deep sigh. Standing up, I transformed into a wolf.

Mr. Needle studied me, intently. I felt like a lab rat.

"I know this is hard for you, Eddie," he said. "But this is how you learn. Through experience. Are you ready?"

Yeah, what do you want me to do?

"Wolves are different from cats. I want you to use your sense of smell. Smell anything?"

A wolf's sense of smell was so much better than a human's... I smelled all kinds of things, even my stinky shoes on the floor. The smells were overwhelming.

"Wolves rely on scent to help them find food and recognize animals. You may have to use this sense one day for other challenges... So." He clasped his hands together. "I want you to come to me."

I hurried to him.

"Eddie, I have a piece of candy in my pocket." He took out the wrapped candy. "I want you to smell it."

I did.

"Scent is like a memory, Eddie. When you're outside, there will be all kinds of smells that you wouldn't normally notice in your human form. Scent will be easier for you to track if it's stationary, like on a sidewalk. But if the wind is carrying it, you will lose the scent. I am going to test you to see how well you do by hiding this piece of candy in this room. I'm going to send you into the hall now. When I'm ready, I'll call you in."

Mr. Needle opened the classroom door and sent me out. Shutting the door behind me, I waited in the hall. A moment later, he opened it back up.

"Okay, Eddie, I'm ready."

Entering the room, the different smells hit me. But then I caught a whiff of the candy. But I wasn't sure where it was.

"Try to imagine that you're playing Marco Polo," said Mr. Needle. "That the candy is calling to you. And don't give him any hints, Dori. Remember this is a learning experience. So, Eddie, focus your attention on that one smell."

I followed his instructions, until I found the candy at the back of the room.

"Good, grab it and bring it to me."

I did as I was told.

"Thanks, I was saving it for later." He smiled, wiping the slobber off. "Okay, you can turn back."

A moment later, I was my old self again. I grabbed my shoes and put them on.

"Now," said Mr. Needle. "Can either of you tell me what you've learned today."

"Well," answered Dori. "It wasn't enough to transform into a cat. Even though I looked like a cat, I had no idea how to act like one."

"Yeah, that's what I realized as a wolf," I replied.

"So, you guys learned how to use skills," said Mr. Needle.

"Right," answered Dori.

Mr. Needle paced the floor. "It isn't always easy for first time students. You two did alright. In a class of thirty, it's hard to help every student. For some, it's awkward because they come from a family where they're the only shapeshifter. So, they suffer from a lack of self-confidence. But since I only have two students, I'll be able to work with you personally one on one. It's important to study all the animals on this list." He held up our quiz papers. "I'm expecting you to master all these animals someday. But, for now, we'll focus on what you're familiar with and work from there. Do you guys have any questions?"

We shook our heads no.

"Good, class is dismissed."

25

As time passed, Dori and I learned how to master our skills better with the help of Mr. Needle. He drilled us. Over and over he tested us. He even created homemade obstacle courses for us. We would practice running through them as different animals. He tested us on speed. How fast we could run. How fast we could transform between different animals. How far we could jump. He even blind folded us to teach us lessons on trust and guidance.

"Remember," said Mr. Needle. "Remain calm and level headed. You are the brain behind the disguise. You make the animal do whatever you want."

And more than ever, the inn was busy. So much time had passed. People were coming and going due to time off because of the recent Thanksgiving holiday. The celebration was over, but people were still spending time with their families. But, for us, it was a different story.

"You know, I think we should do something different today," said Mr. Needle, sitting in his office chair.

"Different?" questioned Dori.

"Yes, I've really been pushing you. So, I've made a request to your parents."

Dori sat up straight. "About what?"

"About having a field trip. So, pack your things," he said, hopping up. "We're leaving!"

"Where are we going?" I asked. This was so sudden.

"To a wildlife and aquarium museum! It's about an hour from here."

"Do we need to pay you?" asked Dori.

"Nope, the funding has already been taken care of. We should be back at the inn around two. However, if you would like to bring extra money to splurge, you may do so."

"Who's driving us?" I asked.

"Me. We'll be taking my car." He gestured to the door. "Well, come on! Come on! Hop to it! We haven't got all day."

26

We rode with Mr. Needle in his car. It had been a long time since we had been out of the small town. I watched the trees pass us by.

"Are you two comfortable?" asked Mr. Needle. "Do I need to turn the heater up?"

"No, we're good," answered Dori.

"Okay, let me know if you get cold."

I stared at Mr. Needle, and something occurred to me.

"Mr. Needle."

"Yes, Eddie."

"How come you didn't visit your family for Thanksgiving?"

For a moment there was silence.

"Because… I don't have any living family to visit." He stared down the road.

"No living relatives?" said Dori.

"None that I know of… My wife passed away when I was a young man. We never had children, and I never remarried."

"What about siblings?" I asked.

"My little sister didn't live to reach adult hood. She died of cancer before turning eleven."

"Oh, how sad," commented Dori.

There was a long awkward silence. Memories of my parents and brothers flashed through my mind. I suddenly felt depressed…

"How about some music?" asked Mr. Needle, changing the subject. "I hope you guys like the oldies!" He turned on the radio, changing the station, until it landed on a 60's song.

Dori then tried to lighten the mood by lip singing and pretending to jam out with an imaginary guitar. Mr. Needle laughed and joined in by singing.

"Come on, Eddie!" said Dori. "You're missing out on all the fun." She pulled on my arm.

"Hey! Cut it out!"

But it didn't do any good. She jerked me back and forth to the timing of music. Finally, I cracked a smile.

27

We entered the wildlife and aquarium museum to see a giftshop and a front desk.

"We'll do the giftshop last," said Mr. Needle. "But first we better pay before touring."

He paid our entrance fee. A minute later, we were looking at the live exhibits inside. We examined all kinds of animals; birds, fish, insects, snakes, turtles… There was an interesting fact at each display case, and there was an animal art gallery too.

"This is so cool!" I said.

"I know," answered Dori. "We should have field trips more often." She said with pleading eyes to Mr. Needle.

"We'll see." He smiled, cocking his eyes. "I might quiz you over this stuff when we get back."

I let out a groan.

"Just kidding!" He laughed.

It took us almost two hours to get through the whole museum. When we were finished, we looked at the giftshop.

"Check out these insect suckers," said Dori. "This one's got a scorpion inside. Want to try it?" She grinned.

"No thanks," I answered. "I'm good."

I stared at all the neat-looking merchandise and finally picked out a t-shirt to buy. Dori went ahead and bought an insect sucker as a joke.

"I can't wait to show this to my dad," she said. "He'll get a big kick out it."

"I'm about to kick you now," I answered.

She backed away, sticking out her tongue.

"Come on, you two," said Mr. Needle. "It's time to go."

28

On the way back to the inn, Mr. Needle stopped at a restaurant and grabbed us some burgers to eat. We happily munched on our food, until we got home.

"Look what I got, mom." Dori grinned, walking into the dining room. She flashed her insect sucker.

"That's nice, honey," said Mrs. Whimple, wrinkling her nose. "Show it to your father." She then spotted me. "Did you have a good time?"

"Yeah, it was fun," I answered.

"Good." She turned her attention to the dirty, round tables. "Eddie, could you help me clean the tables."

"Sure thing."

"Here's a rag and spray bottle." She handed me the items. "When Dori stops parading around, I'll have her help in the kitchen."

Dori straightened up not long after I started working on the tables. She was soon in the kitchen helping Edith and Grandma Whimple. When I was done wiping down the tables, I was sent to pick up trash that needed throwing away.

"You missed one!" joked Grandpa Whimple, hurrying by.

I rolled my eyes and stared out a window. Most of the leaves had already fallen off the trees. Dori and I spent several days raking them up back in October. But now the grounds looked bare. Turning back to my work, I noticed the fall decorations in the house. Soon they would be taken down. Now that Thanksgiving was out of the way, Christmas was knocking at the door.

29

It was the third week of December, and the weather had turned cold. Snowflakes drizzled to the ground. Dori and I were sitting in wooden rockers on the front porch. We were bundled in our coats, watching the flurries.

"Do you think it will stick?" I asked.

"Only if the ground is cold enough, otherwise it will melt," she answered.

"It appears to be sticking."

We watched a few more minutes, until someone rushed through the front gate, heading our way. The person wore a white, hooded coat. When they reached the porch, they pulled off their hood.

It was a fair-skinned girl around our age. She had blond hair that came down to her shoulders and bright, blue eyes. She carried a brown satchel with her. She stopped right in front of us.

"Have you seen my father?" she asked.

"Who's your father?" asked Dori.

"Cindy, there you are!"

A middle-aged man in a leather coat hurried up the steps behind her. He carried a large, brown suitcase in his hand.

"Where did you go?" asked Cindy.

"I was back there!" He pointed, stopping in front of us. The man examined us for a moment. "My name is Jordon Lou," he said, setting down his luggage. "And this is my daughter, Cindy Lou. Are you guys…?"

"My parents own the inn," interrupted Dori.

"Oh, well then you can help us," answered Mr. Lou. "We have reservations."

"Ah," said Dori, getting up from her chair. "Follow me!"

Dori opened the front door and stepped inside. She led them to the front desk.

30

We spotted Cindy, sitting alone at one of the round tables in the dining room. She had a cup of soup in front of her. We hurried over and sat down next to her.

"Hi," said Dori.

She had a vacant stare. It was as if she was in another world, but she raised her head to look at us. At first, she was confused by our presence.

"We didn't introduce ourselves earlier," I said. "My name is Eddie, and this is Dori. Your name is Cindy, right?"

"Yes. Are you two siblings?"

"Cousins," I answered. "I was adopted by the Whimple family."

"Oh."

"How long are you going to stay at the inn?" asked Dori.

"Couple of weeks."

"So, it's just you and your father?" I asked.

"My mom passed away when I was little."

"Oh, I see," I said.

"So, are you here on vacation?" asked Dori.

"Well, kind of... My father's also here on business. It has something to do with..." She paused and stared at us, thinking hard. *Other shapeshifters.*

"Really, other shapeshifters?" I blurted out.

"Eddie!" said Dori, punching me in the shoulder.

"Ouch!"

Cindy laughed. "It's okay. I should have known." She turned her attention to Dori. "Your parents are the ones hosting the meeting, right?"

"I guess so," said Dori. "I overheard them talking about it. They don't tell me about their meetings. It's all top secret."

"I know what you mean," replied Cindy. "My dad can't tell me anything." She remained silent for a moment. "He's one of the teachers at AGT."

"You go to the academy!" said Dori, perking up.

"The Academy of Gifted Teknon," answered Cindy. "I sure do."

"That is so cool!" replied Dori. "I wish I could go…"

Cindy suddenly froze, staring at me and Dori.

"So, then who trains you guys?"

"Mr. Needle," I answered. "He's part of the teaching program."

"Mr. Needle's your teacher?" questioned Cindy.

"Yes, why?"

"Mr. Needle's a legend at the academy."

"Really?" said Dori.

"Oh yeah, there are tons of stories about him. He's considered one of the greatest shapeshifters."

"Wow, I had no idea," I answered.

"Yep, you guys have got to introduce me to him," said Cindy. "Then I can tell all my friends back at the academy that I actually met him."

"Well, okay," I said. "But we should wait until tomorrow morning. He's probably in his room right now, and we shouldn't disturb him."

"You mean, he's here? In this house? Right now?!"

"Yep," answered Dori. "He's been living here since May. We'll introduce you to him when we have class tomorrow."

"You have class tomorrow?"

"From eight to noon," I answered.

"And you're welcome to join us," said Dori. "I'm sure, he won't mind."

31

Sure enough, the next morning, Cindy followed us into our classroom.

"Wow, this is your room," she said. "It's so... roomy." She stared at the two student desk chairs. "You guys are the only students?"

"And you," said Dori, grinning.

"Just for today," she replied.

"Oh, I see we have an exchange student," said Mr. Needle, suddenly walking into the room. He was joking of course. "You must be Mr. Lou's daughter, Cindy," he said, winking. "I've heard great things about you."

"Me?"

"Yes, from your father. He's says you're doing well at AGT."

Cindy blushed.

"And she says that you're a legend," answered Dori. Her hands were on her hip.

"Oops. My cover's been blown." He smiled.

"So, it's true," I said.

"Possibly," he answered, wiggling his eyebrows. He then looked around the room. "Eddie, do you think you could grab a chair for Cindy?"

"You can snatch one from the library," said Dori. "Dad won't mind."

I left the room and came back shortly with a chair.

"Have a seat," said Mr. Needle. He gestured to Cindy.

She sat down.

"So," said Mr. Needle, plopping in the office chair. "I'm a legend."

"Yes, sir," answered Cindy.

"And would you care to explain?" asked Mr. Needle, wheeling around in his chair.

"I was hoping you would do the honor, sir. I've always heard stories about the murdered children, and how you saved the girl."

"Oh, that story." He stopped his chair, and his faced turned solemn. "Well, then, I guess, I better start at the beginning."

"Beginning?" I said.

"It's a long story," answered Mr. Needle. "It's one of the reasons why I taught at the academy for such a long time."

"So, how come you never told us?" asked Dori.

"Because I didn't want to upset you. When students are first learning to hone their skills…, the last thing they need is fear. And I'm not sure that even Cindy has heard the whole story before."

"Only rumors about how the children were murdered," said Cindy.

"Murdered?" I replied.

"The story that Cindy is referring to is known as The Curse. It happened a long time ago when I was a young man. You see, shapeshifters have often been misunderstood, which is why our skill is kept a secret from the outside world. And many years ago, there was a community that was full of shapeshifters. The normal parents passed their genes down to their children. But they didn't understand that their kids possessed a gift. When their children started transitioning into adults, they had no control over their hormones which caused them to transform into an animal unexpectedly. Their parents were afraid and called it The Curse. All the children in the community who possessed the gift were killed, except one."

"They murdered their own children," I said. I couldn't believe my ears.

Dori's face turned pale, and Cindy appeared just as shocked.

"The girl who didn't die was named Katalina. She noticed there had been a lot of funerals that winter. And a friend of hers even disappeared. Shortly after, Katalina came across a shapeshifter in the woods near her home. But she didn't know it. She thought he was just a normal wolf. The shapeshifter could communicate with her telepathically which is how he knew she possessed the gift. He tried to warn her, but she became afraid and ran away."

"Wow," said Dori.

"Anyway, long story short. Katalina escaped the community. I found her all curled up underneath a tree. When I first noticed her, I thought she was just a normal cat, until I realized she could hear my thoughts."

"What were you doing out there?" asked Cindy.

"At the time, the AGT academy was brand new. It was the second holiday break that I had been on, since I started teaching there. I was told to investigate the area where shapeshifters had been spotted. So, I took a train and traveled. But I had to walk to the community. That's when I discovered the truth. The wolf that Katalina had encountered the day before was actually another teacher from AGT. He had discovered the deaths of the children and came to report. He thought Katalina was murdered too. He said he tried to warn her, but she ran off. He informed me that there were no other children in the area with the gift and told me to leave. So, on the way back to the train station, I found her and took her back with me to the school."

"Wow, what an awful story," said Dori.

"It's really sad," commented Cindy. "I've always heard the rumors… but wow."

"I've had a lot more experiences since then," said Mr. Needle. "And some memories I wish I could forget. It hasn't been easy keeping the academy going, but it's come a long way. And now I hope that this program I'm doing with you two." He gestured to me and Dori. "Will be more widespread. A better way to reach out to others with the gift."

"Well, I think you're doing a great job," I said.

"Thank you, Eddie. And I hope that one day you will use your gift to help others the way I've tried to help you."

"And what about me?" asked Dori.

"Oh. And you too. But, for now, I think we should work on our lesson."

32

I rocked back and forth in the chair, watching the snow fall on the front porch. It was a lot thicker than the day before, and it came down in huge clumps. There was at least three inches of snow, glazing the entire area. Sitting there, I heard the front door open. It was Dori.

"Eddie, what are you doing?" she asked. "I thought you were with Cindy."

"I was, but she went up to her room. I think, she's sleeping. Why, what's wrong?"

She glanced around to make sure no one was watching. "A man named Brutus Donnellin checked in today."

"So?"

"So, I overheard him talking with a guest. He says he's a werewolf hunter."

"Really?" I sat up straight. "I didn't realize people actually believed in werewolves."

"They do. And this particular man claims that werewolves don't transform on full moon nights. That it was invented to keep hunters like him… from tracking them down."

"Really?"

"Yes, he said once you're bitten by a werewolf, you become a wild beast. And anyone who has been bitten is doomed. He believes that there is no cure, and the werewolf must be destroyed."

"Well, it's a good thing we're not werewolves," I said, rocking.

"But that's just it."

"What?"

"We're shapeshifters!"

"So?"

"So, don't you think it's strange that a werewolf hunter is staying at this particular inn?"

I stopped rocking. "Now that you mention it, it is kind of strange. Did you tell your parents?"

"Well, I tried to tell mom. But she was busy, cleaning the kitchen…"

"I wouldn't worry about it then. It's not like we're going to do anything."

"True, but you never know…"

"Come on, let's find Cindy," I said, changing the subject. "Maybe she's done taking her nap."

33

We hurried to the second floor where Cindy was staying. Her room was in the middle of the hall. I knocked on the door and listened. But I couldn't hear anything. So, I knocked louder. But there was no noise of any kind.

"I don't think she's in her room," I said. "Maybe she's in the dining room."

"I doubt she's in there," answered Dori. "It's past lunch and way too early for dinner. However, it never hurts to check."

We hurried to the dining room and found it empty.

"How about one of the lounge rooms," I suggested.

"Right, most of the guests hang out there."

"Right."

We searched the lounge rooms but no such luck.

"That's weird," said Dori, thinking to herself. "I wonder where she is…" She then looked at me. "Do you think she and her father checked out of the inn?"

"No, because we would have seen her."

"Well, she's got to be around here somewhere."

"Maybe she's in her room and just couldn't hear me knocking."

Dori shot me a look.

"What? I make mistakes!"

We hurried up the staircase to the second floor and bumped into Oliver. He was heading down the stairs. I could tell he was in a good mood. He was humming a tune to himself.

"Hey, Uncle Oliver!" said Dori. "Have you seen Cindy?"

"Who?"

"Mr. Lou's daughter. She's around our age. Has blond hair…"

"Oh yeah, yeah, yeah. I know who you're talking about."

"Great," said Dori. "Have you seen her?"

Oliver thought for a moment. But then his eyes lit up.

"Yes, I think so," he answered. "I'm pretty sure, I saw her outside."

"Outside?" I said.

"Yeah, I saw her out the window, walking around out back."

"Okay, thanks!" said Dori. "Come on!" She pulled me down the stairs.

34

We stood on the front walk.

"That's weird," said Dori.

"What?"

"No footprints."

"Well, he said she was out back."

"Right, let's go."

We rushed to the backside of the house to see Cindy bundled up in a coat. Noticing us, she paused in her tracks.

"Hey guys!"

"Hey, Cindy," I said, approaching. "What are you doing out here?"

"Well," she answered, biting her lip. "I was just going for a walk."

"How come we didn't see you go out the front door?" asked Dori, coming up.

"Because…" She glanced around, anxiously. "Because I climbed out the window."

"You what?" I said.

"I climbed out the window."

"Why?" asked Dori.

"Because I didn't want him to see me."

"Who?" I asked.

"That guy. Brutus Donnellin."

"The werewolf hunter?" I said.

"Yeah, he gives me the creeps." She stared at the inn. "Is there someplace quiet we can go?"

"How about the woods?" asked Dori. "My parents own most of the land around here."

"Okay, sounds good," answered Cindy. "As long as we're back before nightfall."

We scurried into the woods nearby. The edge of it was laced in icy snow. I could see little icicles, forming on the trees.

"So," I said, hitting a snow-covered branch. "What's up with this Brutus Donnellin?"

"Well, I wasn't going to tell anybody," answered Cindy. "But, I guess, I better…"

"Is it serious?" asked Dori.

"I'm not sure." Her eyebrows furrowed. "You see, awhile back I went on a skating trip with a group of friends. I accidently transformed into a husky. I was pretty sure nobody saw me. But… then I remember seeing that man, Brutus Donnellin."

"You think, he saw you?"

"I don't know. But it seems like every time I leave the school grounds, he's there, following me. And then when he showed up at the inn today… I just had to get away."

"Did you tell your father?" I asked.

"I wanted to, but I thought I was just being paranoid. You know how sometimes you think you see someone you recognize, and then it turns out to be somebody else. But now I'm convinced that he is following me."

We marched across the snowy ground but stopped short in our tracks. There was a loud noise, but it wasn't from an animal.

"What was that?" I asked.

"It sounded like a gunshot," said Cindy.

Listening, we heard it again. It was in fact gunfire and coming from behind us. My whole body froze. A bullet whizzed past me. *Whoa! Somebody's shooting at us!*

"Get down!" said Dori.

But Cindy stumbled over a rotten log, hitting a tree. She rolled down a small hill.

More bullets zipped by us, and we scattered. I couldn't see a thing. Snow was hitting my face. After a minute, the firing stopped.

Trudging around, I scanned from tree to tree, searching for Dori and Cindy. *Where are they?* I tried to remain calm. For a few minutes, I crouched on the ground and waited. Finally, I spotted someone.

"Cindy?"

I hurried to her. I was relieved that she wasn't hurt after all.

"Cindy! Are you okay?"

But then I noticed something was wrong. Her blue eyes were glowing bright red. I heard a low growl escape her lips. And it was not a friendly sound.

"Uh… Cindy."

A second later, she transformed into a white wolf.

"Uh oh."

With a tingling sensation, I became a wolf and took off. Cindy charged after me.

Aaaaaa! That's what I was thinking.

Eddie, what's wrong? It was Dori telepathically communicating with me. *I can hear you yelling in your head.*

It's Cindy! Something's wrong with her. She's chasing me!

I needed to lose her, but I couldn't see where I was going. If I stopped, Cindy would tear me to shreds for sure. *What am I going to do?*

Hang on, Eddie! I'm coming!

And that's when I saw it, a low limb. It was my answer. With a tingling sensation, I transformed from a wolf to a cat. Snarling, Cindy snapped at my feet, but I leaped onto the limb, scampering up the tree.

At the base of the tree, Cindy snarled, baring her teeth. Drool poured from her mouth. I didn't want to attempt a larger transformation. And I certainly didn't want to hurt Cindy. I knew she didn't know what she was doing. *So, what should I do?* I spotted a neighboring tree and leaped to it. I safely landed on a tree branch.

35

While I traveled from tree to tree, Cindy finally lost interest in me and scampered away, chasing a squirrel. I landed on the forest floor, changing back to my normal self. I was safe for the moment. But where was Dori? *Dori! Dori!* I telepathically called. But she was too far away to hear my thoughts. Scanning around, I noticed the snowfall was picking up. I whirled around.

"Oof!" I said, smacking into a figure.

I flew backwards, falling to the ground. When I could focus again, I saw who it was that I had crashed into. It was Brutus Donnellin, and he had a rifle pointed at me. At the sight of the gun, I closed my eyes, waiting for him to pull the trigger. But he didn't shoot.

Instead I heard a howl as Cindy came crashing out of the woods. She was rushing toward me. Right when I thought she would reach me, the man pulled out a whistle and blew on it. In doing so, he made the whistle tweet several times. Cindy stopped in her tracks.

"Get up!" said the man. "Your friend is under my control."

"You're not going to kill me?"

"I never intended to kill you. Just to scare you, so I could get to her." He pointed at Cindy. "I drugged her. She's under my control, until it wears off, which will be…" He pulled out his cellphone. "a few more minutes. But that won't matter, because I'll soon have her hide."

"Why?"

"Because she's a werewolf, and I'm a hunter. And soon… you won't even remember this conversation."

"But I thought you… said… that you… weren't going to kill me."

"I'm not." He grinned, pointing his gun at me. "Don't move, or I will kill you."

We heard a low growl, but it wasn't coming from Cindy.

"Don't move," said Brutus.

The hair on the back of Cindy, bristled. And she started snarling. A flash of grey whizzed by. Brutus pointed his gun and fired. There was silence. He stared into the woods, searching through the snowfall. That's when he was jumped from the side by something large, spotted, and white. It took me a moment to realize that it was a snow leopard. It had to be Dori. But how did she get from over there to here?

The cat sliced at Brutus's hand, causing him to drop the rifle. While he was preoccupied, I snatched the gun. Cindy, who was still in a trance, suddenly woke up. It took her a few seconds, but she realized she was a wolf.

What's going on? Asked Cindy, telepathically.

You were drugged. I answered. *And Dori's fighting Mr. Donnellin.*

No, I'm not.

A bobcat appeared next to us.

Then... who's that? I asked.

The snow leopard pinned Brutus to the ground and knocked him out. A second later, the cat transformed. The girls converted back to their normal selves as well.

"Of course," said Dori, brushing snow off. "I should have known."

Mr. Needle stood next to Mr. Donnellin. He turned and looked at us.

"Are you three alright?" he asked. "Eddie, where's your shoes?"

My socks sank into the snow. I had been too afraid to care.

"I… I guess, I lost them. They usually fall off when I transform."

"No matter," commented Mr. Needle. "Let's get back to the inn."

"What about him?" asked Cindy, pointing.

Brutus Donnellin lay unconscious on the ground.

"Don't worry about him," said Mr. Needle. "He'll be taken care of. I'll send word as soon as we get back to the inn."

36

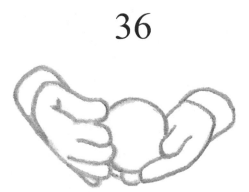

When we got back to the inn, Mr. Needle contacted someone about Brutus.

"Stay here," said Mr. Needle. "I don't want you following me into the woods. Mr. Donnellin is dangerous. He may not be unconscious when I find him again."

He left the inn with Oliver and Mr. Whimple. The rest of the family waited patiently for their return. There was now almost seven inches of snow on the ground.

"Why don't you children go out and play in the snow," said Mrs. Whimple. She bit her lower lip. "But stay in the front. I don't want you near the back where the woods are."

"But I don't have any shoes," I said. "I lost my good pair, and I threw my old ones away months ago."

"You can borrow Mr. Whimple's boots," she answered. "I'll get them for you."

Mrs. Whimple came back with a pair of grey boots for me. I slipped them on and went outside with the girls.

"What do you think they'll do to Mr. Donnellin when they find him again?" asked Cindy, kicking a snow clump.

"I wouldn't worry about it," answered Dori. "They'll take care of it. Come on!" And she made a snowball, throwing it at her.

"Hey!"

And before I knew it, I was stuck in the crossfire of a snow fight. Snowballs whizzed past my head. *Aaaaa! There are too many of them!*

"Eddie, get out of the way!" said Dori.

Too late! I was bombarded with snowballs. *That does it...*

"Aaaa! Look out!" said Cindy. "It's the walking Eddie!"

And during that blissful moment, we forgot all about Brutus Donnellin. Thirty minutes later, we were back inside the house. We changed out of our wet clothes into dry ones. It was a little after five. When we were all cleaned up, we hung out in a lounge room.

We sat on a couch in front of a coffee table. The girls were engaged in a checker game. Dori jumped Cindy's checker piece.

"Whoa, didn't see that coming," said Cindy.

"Ha!" answered Dori.

But then Cindy turned the game around and jumped two of her pieces. She now had a king.

"Grampa Whimple is not going to be happy about this," muttered Dori.

Cindy chased Dori's checker piece around with her king. And after a long battle, Cindy came out on top. Dori gave a pouty face.

"Don't feel bad," said Cindy. "I usually play checkers with my dad."

Mrs. Whimple poked her head into the room.

"Cindy, your father wants you."

"Oh, okay." Cindy hopped off the couch. "I'll see you guys later."

Cindy left the room, and Mrs. Whimple beckoned with her finger.

"You two can help in the kitchen."

37

We hung out with Cindy during the rest of the week until her vacation was over. It was hard to see her leave, but it was time for her to go back to the academy.

"Here's my cellphone number, if you want to get in contact with me," said Cindy. She handed a piece of paper to us. Dori took it. "My dad and I plan on visiting next year."

"Thanks," said Dori. "It was nice meeting you."

"Yeah," I answered. "Glad you came."

And just like that, Cindy and her father walked out the door. We followed them onto the front porch and waved goodbye. Standing there, I felt sad. How easy it was to make friends at the inn and let them go as quickly as they arrived. It just didn't seem fair, but that's the way it was. I then thought about

my parents and brothers. I missed them…
Suddenly I felt a jab.

"Hey!"

Dori pointed at the window behind us. A
freckly, red-haired girl was peeking at us
through the curtain. She looked about nine
years old.

"Who's that?" I asked.

"I don't know, but she's been watching
us," answered Dori. "Come on!"

We rushed inside. The girl took off but
bumped into Aunt Edith.

"Watch it, honey," said Edith, brushing
back her blond hair. "We don't want
accidents."

"S…s…sorry."

"That's alright." She straightened herself.
"What's your name?"

"It's…" She stared at us. "Elina."

"Nice to meet you, Elina. Enjoy your stay
at the inn."

Edith left the area, and Dori grabbed the
girl by the arm.

"Come on, Elina," said Dori, clamping her
hand over the girl's mouth. "You're coming
with us!" She dragged her all the way to the
third floor, so we could talk in private. Dori

finally let go of her arm when we got into the hall. Elina was scared and timid.

"Please, don't hurt me," she said.

"We won't, unless you answer some questions," answered Dori, blocking her way.

"Dori Whimple!"

We turned to see Mr. Needle. He had just come out of his room.

"Mr. Needle," I said. "We didn't mean…"

"There's one thing I won't tolerate and that's bullying," he said.

"But she's been spying on us!" replied Dori.

Elina then fainted, collapsing to the ground. Mr. Needle rushed over and revived her.

"Please, please don't hurt me," said Elina, waking up. She was propped up against the wall.

"Now why would I do that?" asked Mr. Needle, trying to calm her down.

"Because I know…"

"Know what?"

"That you can turn into animals."

How could she possibly know? I thought.

"It doesn't matter," said Mr. Needle. He turned his attention to her. "What's your name, dear?"

"Elina Conner."

"Miss Conner, I'm not going to hurt you. But I want you to promise me one thing."

"What's that?"

"That you won't tell anyone."

38

Mr. Needle brought Elina to the library and had her sit down on a chair in front of a table.

"Dori," said Mr. Needle, standing next to Elina. "Why don't you bring us some hot chocolate?"

Dori left the room.

"Eddie, please sit," gestured Mr. Needle. There was an empty chair beside Elina.

I obeyed and sat down, but I felt awkward.

"Are you going to kick me out of the inn?" asked Elina, lowering her eyes.

"Now why would I do that?" asked Mr. Needle.

"Because I know you guys are different."

"No different than you." He smiled. "We just happen to have a unique gift."

"Turning into animals."

"Yes."

"I think that's so cool!" Her eyes lit up.

"You do?" I questioned.

"Sure, I wish I could do that." She stared at her shoes, blushing. She wouldn't even look us in the eyes. "I wish I could become an animal whenever I wanted."

"But you don't need to," I said.

"Why?"

"Why?" I thought for a moment. "Because... because you're perfect the way you are. You're way better than any old animal."

She smiled.

Dori entered the room, carrying a tray of hot chocolate. She set it down on the table in front of us. There was enough for everyone.

"Dori," said Mr. Needle. "Is there something you'd like to say to Miss Conner." He shifted his glasses, smiling at her. His hands were clasped together.

"Ah, yes... I'm sorry." She gave an apologetic look. "I guess, I got carried away. I didn't mean to scare you."

"Yeah, we're really sorry," I added. "It hasn't been easy."

"What do you mean?" asked Elina.

"Well, sometimes… people can be mean because of our gift," I answered.

"Really?"

"Yeah," I said. "Which is why you would be doing us a big favor if you didn't tell anyone about what we can do. It'll be our secret."

"Okay."

"Come on," said Mr. Needle. "Why don't we all go downstairs. I'm sure, your parents are wondering where you are."

We left the library and went to the first floor. Sure enough, her parents were searching for her. They were relieved to see she was alright. After she was reunited with her family, Mr. Needle called me and Dori to the side.

"We all need to be very careful," he said, whispering. "Remember this is an inn. I know it's hard for you two. But this situation could have gotten out of hand. Do you understand?"

We nodded.

"Yeah, we understand," answered Dori.

"Good, I don't want any more trouble. I'll see you two later."

Mr. Needle left us, hurrying back to the third floor.

39

Things calmed down after Christmas, and our lessons carried on as usual. On a good note, Mr. Needle gave me a new pair of shoes. So, I didn't have to borrow Mr. Whimple's boots anymore. Other than that, we helped around the inn a lot. It would seem our adventures were over for a while, but I couldn't be more wrong.

"Look at this!" said Grandpa Whimple. He held the local paper out to Grandma Whimple.

They were sitting at a round table in the dining room. Dori and I happened to be passing by.

Grandma Whimple glanced at the newspaper article. "Oh dear, it's those ruffians again, the Decayers. They sure are causing a lot of trouble."

"This time they vandalized a cemetery," said Grandpa Whimple, pulling his mustache. "They spray painted their logo all over the tombstones."

"Isn't that a shame," said Mrs. Whimple, overhearing. She walked over to the table to read the paper. "You'd think they would've stopped those hooligans by now."

"Let's just hope they don't start causing trouble here," replied Grandpa Whimple.

I then hurried out of the kitchen.

"And where do you think you're going?" asked Dori, grinning. She quickly caught up with me.

"To take a quick look at my study guide," I answered, rushing up the stairs. "Did you study?"

"Yep."

Today was our science test. I wasn't looking forward to it. Mr. Needle said I was doing fine in class, but I hated tests. For some reason, I'm not very good at answering multiple choice questions, especially if they're tricky.

I entered my room and grabbed my study guide off the bed. A moment later, I was in the classroom, scanning the paper. Mr. Needle entered the room shortly after.

"Ah, I see my students are doing some quick studying," he said, wiggling his eyebrows. "Well, before I pass out your test papers, I would like to read you an announcement."

We sat up straight in our chairs. *Announcement!?*

Mr. Needle cleared his throat as he read from a paper.

"We have personally been invited to the annual AGT (Academy of Gifted Teknon) Track and Field Day. It will be held on May 11th. It will include running, jumping, and catching. It's a special time at the end of the year for students to demonstrate their skills." He leaned forward. "That means metamorphosis," he whispered.

"But won't someone see," I said.

"It's held inside a huge gymnasium," he answered. "There is high security there to protect shapeshifters."

"How will we get in?" asked Dori.

"First, there's registration. With your parent's permission, I will have you registered. After we're on record, we'll have to go through a human scanner."

"A what?" I asked.

"Before we can enter the gymnasium, a doorman will have us walk through a scanner. It's designed to detect the mutant gene in your body. It will go off on a normal person."

"But what if you have normal parents?" I asked.

"Well, there are exceptions. A parent should be on school record for allowing their child to attend. They must then prove that they are aware of their child's gift and provide valid proof that they are who they claim to be."

"That sounds awful," said Dori.

"Well, it has to be that way to prevent shootings. Shapeshifters have often been persecuted in the past."

"What about money?" asked Dori.

"Don't worry about that right now."

"Why?" I asked.

"Because." He wiggled his eyebrows. "It's time for your test."

40

After we were done taking our test, Mr. Needle had us read a story while he graded our papers. Thirty minutes later, we went over the test questions together. While we were doing so, we heard commotion outside the room.

"Uh oh," said Mr. Needle. "I wonder what's going on?" He craned his neck. "You two stay here." He hopped up from the office chair and left the room.

Dori leaned over in her chair. "Let's go check it out."

"Dori, he told us to stay here."

"Come on, you're not going to miss out on the action. Are you?"

We scurried out of the room into the hall. We didn't see a soul in sight.

"Something must have happened downstairs," said Dori.

We snuck to the first floor to see a circle of people. One of the windows in a lounge room was shattered. Glass covered the floor. The Whimple family rushed to clean it up.

"Ahem!" Mr. Needle approached us. "I thought, I told you two to stay in the room."

Dori grinned.

"What happened?" I asked.

"Someone broke a window," he answered.

"Who?" asked Dori. "One of the Decayers?"

"Upstairs," said Mr. Needle, motioning with his hand. "Not here." He looked at several visitors. "We'll talk in the classroom." He ushered us.

When we were back in the room, he spoke.

"I can see that it's hard to keep a secret from you two. But to answer your question earlier," he said, staring at Dori. "It was in fact the Decayers."

"The local ruffians," I said.

"Oh, they're more than that," he answered. "The Decayers didn't originate around here."

"They didn't?" said Dori.

"I can see your parents left you in the dark. And I'm not sure I'm the person that should be telling you. But you'll find out sooner or later."

"Find out what?" asked Dori.

"It's no accident the inn was targeted. The Decayers are starting trouble for a reason."

"Why?" I asked.

"Because they're shapeshifters."

"Wha!" said Dori.

"It's true. They're led by a group of young adults."

"They?" I questioned.

"Many of them are between the ages of twelve and sixteen. They travel from place to place, scavenging around."

"But I still don't understand why they attacked the inn?" I asked.

"They attacked the inn because they think they're a reformation group."

"Meaning…," said Dori.

"Meaning they believe that anyone who isn't a part of their group is evil. They believe we're immoral, and that they are making changes to improve the situation."

"How does breaking a window improve the situation?" I asked.

"It's their way of making a statement. They don't like that your parents allow the inn to be open to non-shapeshifters. They want us to be separate from the rest of the world."

"But most normal people don't know shapeshifters exist," said Dori.

"Yes, but you still coexist with them in society, even if they don't know about your gift. The Decayers don't want to be around people without the gift. They believe they're evil because of past persecution. Many of them have been abused."

"Oh, how sad," commented Dori.

"Yes. So, they want a separate community away from everyone else who doesn't meet their qualifications. And because we choose to mingle with others in society, they think we're evil." Mr. Needle sat down in his office chair. "This may be hard for you to understand, because you're so young. But many of these children are runaways who want to be accepted. To them, their group is their family."

"So, what's going to happen to the Decayers?" I asked.

"Well, I'm sure, they're long gone by now. They tend to hop around from place to place. It isn't easy to catch them because of their gift. There are shapeshifters who handle situations like this. But the only thing we can do is report them."

"You don't think they'll attack the inn again?" asked Dori.

"No, not unless they want to be apprehended. That's probably why their group has survived so far. They never stay in the same place."

"Actually, I feel sorry for them," I said, suddenly thinking about my uncle.

"Why?" questioned Dori.

"Do you remember the first time we met?"

"Yes." She smiled. "It was the first time I ever saw a wolf upside down."

I rolled my eyes. "But do you remember why I was running away."

"You… said you thought your uncle was chasing you."

"Well, I thought he was." My face turned scarlet.

Mr. Needle's eyebrows shot up.

"Anyway, I was thinking about how he abused me. He was a person with the gift, but he wanted to use me. He literally imprisoned me in a room, because he didn't want me to escape."

"How come you never explained this before?" asked Dori.

"Dori!" said Mr. Needle.

"It's okay," I answered. "But I was thinking about how hard it is to forgive someone who's hurt you. I know he's dead, and he can't hurt me anymore. But when I think about him, there's still…"

"Resentment," replied Mr. Needle.

"Yeah, so I can kind of see from the Decayers point of view. They've been mistreated."

"So, what's the difference between you and them?" asked Mr. Needle.

For a moment I was quiet. I gave a sigh. "I suppose, it has to do with what my mom said when she was alive. When my siblings and I fought, she would always say Two Wrongs Don't Make A Right. But until today it never clicked. Just because someone mistreats you, doesn't make it right for you to hurt others. Not that I go around hurting people, but…"

"It's hard not to hit someone who's being mean to you," finished Mr. Needle.

"Wait a second," said Dori. "Are the Decayers hurting innocent people?"

"Not that I know of," said Mr. Needle. "No one has been physically harmed yet, but they certainly are making a fuss. I just hope the situation doesn't get worse. What if they had set the inn on fire?"

My face turned pale.

41

Sure enough, the Decayers were gone. But their surprise attack upset the Whimple household. Other than that, Dori received a message from Cindy Lou. She wanted to know how we were doing. Dori answered her back about our recent experience.

"Come on," said Dori. "Mom wants us to go to the store." She pushed me out the front door.

"What is it this time?" I asked.

"Salsa, she says it's for her special recipe. Anyway, she told us to stay together. Even though there hasn't been a sighting of the Decayers. She doesn't want us to take any chances."

"But, Dori, it looks like it's going to rain," I said, staring at dark, grey clouds. "Couldn't we ask Mr. Needle to give us a lift?" I pointed at him through the window.

"No time for that!" And she jerked my arm.

About six minutes later, we were at the store.

"Hey, wait up!" I said.

"Eddie, would you please keep up!"

Dori turned to look at me. She almost tripped over a scrawny guy.

"Oh, sorry!" said the man. "I didn't mean to get in your way."

The little man sped away. When he was gone, it suddenly occurred to me something wasn't right.

That's weird.

What's weird? Asked Dori, telepathically.

The store seems empty.

She looked around for a moment. *You're right! Come on, let's get out of here!* Dori then handed me several jars of salsa.

We hurried to the manager, who was working a cash register. She had dyed, blond hair and piercing blue eyes.

"Wha, you mean you two are still here?" she said.

"What do you mean?" asked Dori.

"I'm about to close up shop."

"Why?" I asked.

"Look!" She pointed out the window.

A sheet of rain poured to the ground.

"There's a storm coming," she said, ringing up the salsa. "When the lightning gets bad, I have to close the registers down. This is the only one open."

We heard thunderclap.

"You can stay here, until the storm passes," she said.

But Dori didn't want to. She paid for the salsa, and we scurried out. A second later, we stood under the store's roof overhang. I watched the trees sway in the wind. Lightning crashed to the ground.

"Dori, I think you should call your dad to pick us up," I said.

"I think, you're right," she answered, pulling out her cellphone. She quickly phoned her dad.

Shortly after, I heard sirens. Dori's cellphone kept sending her tornado alerts. A second later, a car pulled up.

"Look, Dori! It's Mr. Needle."

A huge tree then crashed to the ground, splitting. A limb hit Dori, and she became trapped under it.

"Eddie!"

Blood dripped down the side of her face where a limb scratched her. Mr. Needle hopped out of the car, while I tried to pull Dori out.

Dori struggled under the weight, but I couldn't get her out. Her eyes began to swell.

"Dori," said Mr. Needle, rushing up. "Don't cry."

"But I'm stuck!"

"Dori, look at me."

She turned her head.

"Remember you have a gift! Use it!"

"But what about the store manager?"

"Don't worry about her," said Mr. Needle, watching the manager through the glass window. "Eddie will cover for you." He motioned for me to go in the store to distract the woman.

I opened the glass door, bumping into the manager.

"Is that girl alright? Do I need to call…?"

"She's fine," I interrupted.

"But she's…"

"Look!" I said, pointing.

"What!?" She turned her head. It was just enough time for Dori to transform into a cat and get herself out from under the tree. When the manager turned back around, she spotted Dori, standing next to Mr. Needle. "Oh good, she's alright."

Dori and Mr. Needle hurried into the store.

42

When we made it back to the house, Mrs. Whimple was hysterical. She rushed to the entranceway.

"Dori, I'm so sorry," she said, grasping her daughter. "I didn't mean to send you and Eddie out into a storm!"

"But you didn't," said Dori. "It wasn't storming when we left the inn."

But Mrs. Whimple wouldn't listen.

"Mom, you can let me go now. I need to breathe."

"Oh. Sorry, dear." She released her. "I just can't believe a tree limb fell on you."

"Now that's what I call good genes," said Grandpa Whimple, winking. "Only a Whimple can survive getting hit by a tree."

Mrs. Whimple scowled, but the rest of the family laughed, including Mr. Needle.

"Dear, you shouldn't say things like that," said Grandma Whimple. "She could have been killed."

"Did you guys hear about the touchdown tornado?" asked Uncle Oliver, suddenly.

"No, where was it?" asked Mr. Needle.

"About three miles away from the store."

My eyes widened.

"That's right," said Oliver. "You guys were lucky."

"Well, I'm just glad nobody got hurt," replied Aunt Edith, fluffing her blond hair.

"Me too," answered Mrs. Whimple. "And I hate to say it, but it's time to fix supper." She stared at me and Dori. "Thank you so much for bringing the salsa! I'll be sure to make you guys a special treat."

"What! You mean, I don't get a special treat," said Oliver, pouting.

"A tree limb didn't fall on you, sonny," answered Grandpa Whimple.

"Better luck next time," answered Mr. Whimple, patting his shoulder.

"Boys, boys!" said Mrs. Whimple. "There'll be plenty of food for everyone. Now back to work!"

43

A snake slithered underneath my chair. I was in the kitchen about to eat breakfast when I noticed it slip in through the backdoor. Thinking fast, I knew I had to get it out of the house. I wasn't afraid of snakes, but I knew for a fact Mrs. Whimple was. Knowing her, she'd snatch a cake server and beat the tar out of it.

I seized a glass jar off a table and scooped up the snake. Lifting it up, I peered at it and watched it wriggle inside.

"Cool, where did you get it?"

I jumped. I didn't even know Dori was behind me. "I found it under my chair," I answered.

"Really? Let me show it to mom." She reached for the jar.

"No way! This snake is going outside."

"Party pooper."

A moment later I released it outside and was back in the house. Dori was eating breakfast. She grinned at me.

"Ready to start your Monday morning," she said.

"I've already started it." I glared. *I don't trust you. Something's up your sleeves.*

She quickly rolled up her sleeves and grinned. *You forgot, didn't you?*

"Forgot what?"

"That today's our shapeshifting test."

"No, I didn't forget. I'm just… trying not to think about it. I spent last night practicing in my room."

"Are you nervous?"

"Are you?"

"Yep. If we don't do good, it will affect our scholarship funds."

My eyes went wide.

"No worries, I think, we'll do alright."

But I could tell she wasn't sure. About ten minutes later, we were in the classroom. Mr.

Needle walked into the room. He plopped down in the office chair.

"You two arc quiet today," he said, peering at us through his glasses.

"We're just waiting," answered Dori.

"For your test. Take a deep breath and breathe."

We cracked a smile.

"Are you guys ready?"

We nodded.

"Now remember. Both of you must transform into every single animal that you've been studying. Depending on how well you transform, depends on what kind of grade you get. Is everybody clear on that?"

We nodded.

"Good. Dori, you may begin."

44

After our test, we played Pictionary on the board while Mr. Needle added up our scores.

"What, that's not a monkey," said Dori. "Looks more like a pig."

I shot her a dirty look. "It's your turn."

"Enough of that you two," said Mr. Needle. "Sit." He pointed at our chairs.

We obeyed. Dori stuck her tongue out at me.

"Ahem," said Mr. Needle, trying to keep a straight face. "Now that I have your undivided attention, I want you to know that you both passed with A's."

"Really?" I said, perking up.

"Yep, you've both improved greatly since the beginning of the year. Soon your training will be over. You will have one more shapeshifting test to pass."

"Will it be like the test we just took?" asked Dori.

"No, this will be a written test. A review over everything we have discussed in class about metamorphosis."

I sank in my chair. *I hate tests like that...*

"I will give you both a study guide to help you later. Other than that, class is dismissed."

We got up from our seats and left the room. Dori and I speed walked against each other down the hall. And soon we were on the first floor, heading to the dining room.

"Hey, wait a second," said Dori, stopping.

"What?" I bumped into the back of her.

"Look!" She pointed.

A young woman was talking to Mr. Whimple at the front desk. She was tall, thin, and had short, black hair. She wore a black shirt that matched her black, skinny jeans and shoes.

"So, it's just a guest."

"No, listen!"

"You say you've just moved here," said Mr. Whimple, eyeing the woman with his gold specs.

"Yes, my name is Ivy Cypris. I live a quarter of a mile away."

"You do?"

"Yes, I just moved into the old house across Drowsy Road."

"Really? I thought that house would never sell. The old woman who used to live there was very sweet."

"Yes, well I'm glad I bought the place. Anyway, I just came over to introduce myself."

"I see. Well, it's a pleasure to meet you. Feel free to drop by the inn in case you need any help."

"Oh yes, thank you."

Ivy rushed by us and left the inn.

"Dori? Is something wrong?" I asked.

"It's just… she's so young. She looks about twenty."

"I'd say twenty-one."

She cocked her eyes at me. "Come on, let's go eat."

45

After we ate lunch, we helped around the inn. But Dori rushed the chores. She was faster than normal.

"Where are you going?" I asked, trailing her.

"Oh, I just thought I'd go for a walk. Do you want to come with me?"

"Okay."

But I had a feeling there was more to it than just a walk.

We stepped outside onto the wet ground. It was cool outside but not cold. The green grass was moist with dew, and our shoes were soaked. Out in the distance, there were blue and grey hills. The birds were chirping. A minute later, we were in the woods.

The smell of cedar trees wafted in the air, and I dunked under a wet branch. However, I scraped against the leaves, getting sprayed with water. Droplets trickled across my forehead, and I wiped the water away.

"Dori, what are we really doing out here?" I asked, crunching down on wet leaves.

"I thought we could cut across the woods and spy on our new neighbor."

"Why?"

"Don't you think it's strange she moved here?"

"No, what's strange about it?"

"Have you forgotten where we are? This is the town of Watalu. There's nothing… out here, except our inn, the gas station, and the general store. Where is she going to work?"

"Well, maybe she works in the town next door."

"Maybe. But it just seems strange. Most of the locals around Watalu are related. She just seems… out of place."

"Wow, Dori, if I didn't know any better. I'd say… that you're being indifferent."

"I am not! I just think it's strange."

"Well, she seems nice to me."

"You don't even know her!"

"True."

"Come on!"

We marched deeper into the woods and approached branch water. We stepped across damp, moss-covered rocks, until we reached the other side. The sound of crows could be heard in the distance.

"Do you hear that?" asked Dori.

"What, the birds?"

"No."

I then heard a low growl... I turned to see a large, black dog, blocking our way.

"Whoa, where did that come from?" I questioned.

"Is it friendly?" asked Dori.

"How am I supposed to know?"

The dog gave a low growl.

"I don't think it's friendly," said Dori.

The dog barked ferociously.

"Let's back away slowly." I instructed.

We did, and the dog did not chase us. When we were at a safe distance, we fled back to the inn.

"That... was... weird," said Dori, catching her breath.

"Yeah, it was," I answered. "Do you think it was a normal dog?"

"No."

"You mean, you think it was..."

"One of the Decayers? Yes."

"So, why not attack us?"

"Probably thought we were normal kids. If we went missing, it would attract too much attention."

"Shouldn't we tell your parents?"

"Not yet. I still want to spy on our new neighbor. But this time we won't go through the woods."

So, we took the long way around. About five minutes later, we were staring at a worn-down, one-story house. The windows looked dusty and dirty.

"It looks empty," I said.

"Excuse me? May I help you."

We jumped. A young woman came up from behind us. It was Ivy.

"You scared us," said Dori, taking a step back.

"I did?"

"Yes, we…"

"Hey, haven't I seen you guys somewhere before?"

"At the inn," I answered.

"Yes, of course..."

Dori shot me a look.

"So, are you guys staying the night there?"

"We live there," answered Dori.

Her eyebrows furrowed. "You live there?"

"Yes, Mr. Whimple is my father."

"I see." She pressed a smile. "Well, I'm your new neighbor. Would you guys care to come in the house for a visit."

"Ye…" I started to say, but Dori elbowed me.

"We can't," interrupted Dori. "Mom and dad are probably wondering where we're at. Maybe some other time. Bye!" She scurried away.

"Dori, slow down!" I hurried to catch up.

When we were a good distance away from Ivy, she skidded to a stop, causing rocks to fly.

"Eddie, don't you get it?" She grabbed me by the shoulders. "She's one of the Decayers. Did you see the look on her face when I told her who my father was?"

"Yes. But remember what Mr. Needle said in class. We have to remain calm and…"

"Level headed," finished Dori. "But if we'd gone inside her house, we would've been trapped for sure."

"You don't think we couldn't have gotten out?"

"Decayers are dangerous. We don't know if she's the only one living inside that place. Let's not take any chances."

"Whoa, back up here."

"What?"

"Where's the old Dori I know. The risk taker?"

"Not this time, Eddie. We need to tell my parents."

And we did. As soon as we reached the house, we told them about our experience in the woods and our suspicions about Ivy.

"What do you think, honey?" asked Mrs. Whimple.

"I don't know," answered Mr. Whimple. "Ivy could very well be one of the Decayers. But we can't just jump to conclusions. We have no proof."

"Isn't our word good enough?" asked Dori, crossing her arms.

"The problem is that you didn't see Ivy transform into the dog," replied Mr. Whimple.

"Grrr…"

"However, I will dispatch a message about a possible sighting of the Decayers," said Mr.

Whimple. "In the meantime, you two are not to leave the inn without my permission."

"What?!" said Dori.

"It's for your own safety."

"That's right," said Mrs. Whimple. "If what you say is true, then we don't want you near her."

46

"Dori, where did you get that?" I asked, standing in the hallway. We were on the third floor.

"Oh this," she said, grinning. She was holding a tiny, tortoiseshell kitten. "I found it."

"You know, you're not supposed to go outside. What if your parents find out?"

She ignored me. "I found the kitten slinking around Ivy's yard. She chased it away with a broom."

"Did she see you?"

"No. I can't believe she'd be so mean to it. It was so scared that it ran into the woods and climbed up a tree. I had to transform just to get it down. I've been feeding it slices of turkey meat."

"Aren't you afraid it will pee on you?"

"No. I filled a box with dirt and put it in my room. So far, she's used the bathroom in it."

I wrinkled my nose.

"It's the first pet I've ever had."

"You've never had a pet before?"

"My parents are always afraid to have pets, because some people have allergies. But I'm going to keep her in my room."

We heard creaking down the hall. It was Mr. Needle.

"Dori Whimple," he said, approaching. "What is that?"

"This." She held the kitten close to her. "Why nothing…"

"Dori…"

She wilted. "Oh, please don't tell. I want to keep her." She showed the kitten to Mr. Needle.

He smiled. "You know, your parents are going to eventually find out about this."

She gave a pleading look.

"But, for now." He tapped his nose. "Mum's the word." And he walked away, whistling.

"Yes!" said Dori.

I shook my head. "Dori, you're terrible." I laughed. "Can I see the kitten?"

"Sure." She handed it to me.

"What are you going to call her?" I petted its soft fur.

"Tilly."

I arched an eyebrow. "Really?"

"Yep."

"That's…. original."

She stuck her tongue out at me. "I think it's pretty."

"Okay, but it's your kitty." I handed it back to her. "So, did you learn anything about Ivy?"

"No." And she hurried into her room.

I was going to follow her but changed my mind. I noticed the study room door down the hall was open. *That's odd?*

What's odd? Asked Dori, telepathically.

She came out of her room.

"Where's the kitten?"

"I put her in the box."

"Oh. Anyway, listen."

We crept to the end of the hall. Mr. Whimple was on his cellphone.

"So, you're not going to send someone to check it out," he said. "Why not?" There was a short pause. "What new sighting?" He waited a moment before speaking. "Are you sure the Decayers were seen there…? I see. Well, I'm sorry to have bothered you. But you can never be too careful. I know. I'll talk to you later."

He ended the conversation, and we rushed down the hall to Dori's room.

"So, a new sighting of the Decayers was seen," said Dori, thinking. "I guess, I was wrong about Ivy."

"Yeah, I guess…" Now I was confused.

"Well, I still don't like her," replied Dori. "She was mean to Tilly. Come on, let's play with the kitten."

47

I climbed out my bedroom window in my pajamas. I wasn't convinced that Ivy wasn't one of the Decayers. Something didn't add up to me. Staring at the sparkling stars in the night sky, I hurried to the woods and transformed into a wolf. When I reached the other side, I stopped. I heard a bark. Listening, I spotted something scurrying towards Ivy's house. It was huge and black. When it turned its head, I realized it was a large dog. The same dog in the woods a few days ago. Then something odd happened. It was as if the dog had changed its shape. It now stood on two legs. A chill ran through my body, and I bolted.

I fled to the inn. Transforming into a cat, I climbed through my bedroom window. I had to find Dori. Tiptoeing into the hall, I rapped on her door.

"Eddie, what are you doing?"

It was Mrs. Whimple. She shined a flashlight at me.

"I... couldn't sleep."

"Did you have a nightmare?" She lowered her light.

"Something like that."

"I've got the munchies. It's hard to sleep when you're hungry. Why don't we go downstairs, and I'll fix you something?"

"Okay."

I followed Mrs. Whimple to the kitchen. She turned on the light when something scurried across her foot. She gasped for breath but then saw Dori. She had a quizzical look on her face when she spotted the kitten on the floor.

"Dooriii, where did this come from?"

"It... just... sort... of... Can I have it?"

"Dori!"

"Please, mom! I'll take good care of it." She snatched the kitten off the floor.

"Look, I'm tired. I'm hungry." She rubbed her forehead. "We'll…"

Dori gave a pleading look.

"We'll… discuss this in the morning."

"So, the kitten can stay," she said, holding it to her chest.

"For now, it can stay in your room."

"Yes!"

"Do you need a box?"

"No, I've already got one."

Her mother gave her a look. "What were you doing in here anyway?"

"Tilly was hungry."

"Well, she's not the only one. Come on, let's see what we can find."

48

I sat in class, trying to listen to Mr. Needle. But my focus was elsewhere. And Dori kept playing with her kitten in the middle of class.

"You know, there's a reason why pets shouldn't be allowed in school," said Mr. Needle, eyeing her with his glasses. He was leaning against the office desk with his arms crossed.

"It's a good thing this isn't a regular school." She grinned, holding her kitten. "Tilly needs extra attention."

Mr. Needle's eyebrows shot up. He then turned his attention to me. "Eddie, are you okay? You look confused."

Did Ivy really transform? Or was I imagining things?

"What did you say?" asked Dori, staring at me.

"I... I didn't say anything."

"We can hear your thoughts," said Dori. "Remember?"

I blushed.

"Is there something you want to tell us?" asked Mr. Needle.

"I... I snuck outside last night," I said, sinking in my chair.

"You what?!" replied Dori. Her jaw dropping.

"I snuck out. I wasn't convinced that you were wrong about Ivy."

"Who's Ivy?" asked Mr. Needle.

"Our new neighbor," answered Dori. "I thought she was one of the Decayers, until..."

"Until we overheard her father talking on his cellphone," I finished. "Someone told him there was another sighting of the Decayers in a different area."

"So, I thought I was wrong about Ivy," said Dori.

"Right, but I wasn't convinced. I decided to investigate myself. I snuck out last night to find out and saw someone transform from a dog into a person. I think..., it was Ivy."

"But you don't know for a fact," responded Mr. Needle.

"No."

"I hate to say it," said Mr. Needle, shaking his head. "But what you did was incredibly stupid. What if some of the guests staying here saw you? Remember the little, red-haired girl, Elina?"

I sank further in my chair. "What should I do?"

"Nothing, for now," said Mr. Needle, rubbing his forehead. "I'm going to open the door and let some air in. I'm suddenly feeling rather hot."

Mr. Needle hopped up and opened the door. But he didn't go out into the hall. He beckoned to me with his hand.

"What is it?" I asked, getting up.

He put his finger over his mouth to silence me. I then peeked my head out the door.

"Who's that young woman at the end of the hall?" He asked, pointing.

She was cautiously examining the hallway, going from door to door. She couldn't get in because the doors were kept locked in case of thieves. But she was trying really hard. So far, she hadn't noticed us yet.

"That's Ivy," I said, whispering.

Mr. Needle pulled me to the side and gently closed the door. He then turned off the light.

"Want me to lock the door?" I asked.

"No. I want you and Dori to move the office desk in front of the window."

"Why?" asked Dori.

"If Ivy really is one of the Decayers, she'll try to escape through it. Be extremely quiet."

We did as we were instructed.

"Now what?" I asked.

"Wait here in the dark. If she comes through the door, I want you to grab her legs. Dori, message your father. Tell him we have an intruder."

Dori pulled out her cellphone and started typing. Several seconds later, Ivy entered the room, and I grabbed her legs.

"Hey!" She said, crashing to the ground.

Mr. Needle closed the door behind her and turned on the lights. Dori stood off to the side, holding her kitten.

"You!" said Ivy, glaring at me.

Mr. Needle motioned to me, and I let go of her.

Ivy stood up, angrily. "What's the meaning of this?"

"Decayers," said Mr. Needle, suddenly.

She flinched.

"So, you are one," said Mr. Needle, watching her expression. "How did you get up here without anyone seeing you?"

"Besides us." I added.

Ivy twisted her fingers, anxiously. Her eyes darted around. She realized we had the window blocked, and her face turned pale. After a moment, she spoke. "I noticed a window on the third floor was open and climbed through it."

My heart skipped a beat. I was so shaken from last night that I forgot to shut my bedroom window.

"Why are you here?" asked Dori.

"Because…" Her eyes shifted. "I thought my cover was blown. When I checked my night camera this morning, I saw a wolf in the woods. Guessing it wasn't a normal wolf, I realized a person was spying on me. So, I decided it was now or never."

"Let me get this straight," said Mr. Needle. "You moved here to collect information."

"Yes, once I got what I needed. I was going to inform the others. It was a great disguise. But now it's pointless." She hung her head. "I have failed."

"Who's your leader?" I asked.

Her eyes pierced into mine. "Me. I didn't want to attract attention. I knew other people would keep chasing my group, so I separated from them. I told them it would be safer."

"Safe?" questioned Dori. "But if you weren't causing trouble, nobody would be after you in the first place."

Ivy rolled her eyes. Shortly after, there was a knock on the door. Mr. Whimple called out to us.

"Are you guys alright?" he asked.

"Yes," answered Mr. Needle. "You can come in."

I opened the door and stood to the side. The rest of the Whimple family entered the room. There was nowhere for Ivy to go.

49

Test Study Guide ?!

After Ivy was taken away, Mr. Needle informed us that she would be questioned about her group's possible whereabouts.

"What makes you think she'll talk?" I asked. Me and Dori were moving the office desk away from the window.

"Well, I'm not sure she will," he answered. "But I hope she does. Maybe through her, they can figure out where her group plans on going next after their recent sighting."

"Well, I'm just glad she didn't pull a knife on us," answered Dori.

"Or a gun for that matter," I replied, thinking about Brutus Donnellin, the werewolf hunter.

Me and Dori set the desk down.

"She couldn't," said Mr. Needle. "Just like how electronic devices don't blend into metamorphosis neither do weapons. It would have simply fallen to the ground if she had transformed. And I imagine that she transformed in order to get through the window on this floor."

"It makes sense," I said.

"Yes, well now that things are back in order," replied Mr. Needle. "I can pass out your test study guide."

We groaned.

"It's for your own good. In several weeks, you'll have to take your last test on shapeshifting. It's important you pass it."

"But what about our other tests?" asked Dori. "You know, those other subjects. English, Math, History, Science, Art...."

"They're important too."

"How important?" I asked.

"Veeery important." He leaned forward. "I expect you to do double studying on them. And... there will also be study guides." He wiggled his eyebrows.

Dori glared, stroking her kitten.

"It's for your own good," he said, giving her a study guide. "Here's yours, Eddie." He handed me mine. "Oh, and one more thing. I forgot to tell you."

"Tell us what?" asked Dori.

"That you're registered."

"For what?" I questioned.

"For the AGT Track and Field Day."

Dori beamed.

"That's right. As soon as we get all your tests out of the way, we'll travel up there."

"What day is it again?" I asked.

"May 11th," he answered.

"Can Tilly come?" asked Dori, holding up her kitten.

"We'll see," said Mr. Needle.

"We might be able to smuggle her in," I replied, whispering.

Mr. Needle shot me a look. "We'll be gone for about three days. It will take us all day to get up there. Once we arrive, they'll provide us with guest housing."

"So, basically we'll drive up there, get one day to explore, and then head back," said Dori.

"Not exactly. Mr. Whimple will drive us to a bus station. Once we reach it, we'll ride the bus the rest of the way."

"Sounds like it's going to be a boring trip," replied Dori. "I better bring my music player."

"Right," I said.

"And I'll bring books," answered Mr. Whimple.

50

About a week later, it was reported that the Decayers had been stopped. They wouldn't be causing any more trouble. On top of that, Dori's birthday rolled around, and she was excited. The family got together around noon to celebrate, even Mr. Needle was there. Mrs. Whimple had a white tablecloth spread over a round table. On it was a cherry, chocolate cake and presents. Dori grinned, sitting in front of the cake. Grandma Whimple placed fourteen birthday candles on it and lit them. We stood around her.

"Fourteen," said Grandpa Whimple, whistling. "Doesn't seem right." He turned to look at me. "You'll be next you know."

"I still have a while to go."

"If I didn't know any better," said Oliver, whispering. "I would have thought you were older."

"I heard that, Uncle Oliver!" answered Dori, sticking her tongue out.

"Look this way!" replied Edith. She was holding a digital camera.

"Smile," said Mrs. Whimple.

"At the rate she's going we'll be here forever," commented Mr. Needle.

"I know what you mean," remarked Mr. Whimple, laughing.

Dori glared, and Edith took a picture.

"I think, we should redo that," said Mrs. Whimple. "Now, honey, try to smile."

After a minute, Edith finally got a good shot of her with the cake. We then sang happy birthday to her, and she opened her presents. She got clothes, a bracelet, and an art kit.

"Here," said Mr. Needle. He handed her a present wrapped in newspaper.

"What is it?" asked Dori.

"Open it and see."

Dori ripped open the paper to see a hand carved animal.

"It's a panther," he answered. "I know how much you like cats, so I got it for you."

Dori held it up. It had a nice wood finish.

"Oh, thank you!" She beamed. "I'll call it Mr. Needle."

"You're naming it after me?"

"Yes, it reminds me of the time you turned into a fat panther."

We burst out laughing.

"I'll be sure to put it on my dresser." Dori took off, running.

51

Two weeks later our tests rolled around, but we survived them. Mr. Needle was pleased with our final grades. And as promised, it was time for our trip to AGT. Dori messaged Cindy Lou about it on her cellphone.

"What did Cindy say?" I asked, holding a brown suitcase. I was standing near the front desk next to Dori.

"That she can't wait to see us," answered Dori. Her suitcase was sitting at her feet. "When we get there, she says she'll show us around."

"Are you two ready?" asked Mr. Whimple, entering the inn. "Mr. Needle's already in the pickup."

"Yes," I answered.

"Are you sure you have everything?" asked Mrs. Whimple, coming up.

"I suppose so," answered Dori. She gave her mother sad eyes and picked up her suitcase.

"I'm sorry, but Tilly cannot go with you," said Mrs. Whimple. "Now give me a hug. And don't worry, I'll take good care of her."

Dori nodded, grasping her.

Mrs. Whimple got a little teary eyed and let go of Dori. "I want you to have fun. Call me when you get there." She waved goodbye to us.

Shortly after, we were off. While Mr. Whimple drove, he talked about his years at AGT Academy.

"Wait a second," said Dori. She was sitting in the back with me. "You mean to tell me that you were his teacher." She stared at Mr. Needle.

"Dori, I told you that I was a teacher at AGT," said Mr. Needle.

"I know that. I just didn't know that you taught dad."

Mr. Needle chuckled.

"I think, when I was in school, it was a requirement to have Mr. Needle as a teacher," said Mr. Whimple.

"Why? Did Mr. Needle teach every subject?" asked Dori, eyeing him.

"No, but it sure felt like it." He looked at us in the review mirror.

"Did you ever get in trouble?" I asked.

"Many times," answered Mr. Whimple. "Mostly because of my brothers. If it weren't for them, I probably wouldn't have ended up in detention so much."

"What for?" asked Dori.

"Stupid stuff."

"Like what?" I asked.

"Oh… well, one time we thought it would be funny to stand on our chairs in the cafeteria and read corny love poems to the most popular girls in school. That got us some dirty looks for sure. I got jerked off the chair by Mrs. Edaline. I received a whole week's worth of detention."

"Wow, dad. Does mom know?"

"Actually, that's how I met your mom. In detention."

"What was she doing in detention?" asked Dori.

"Yeah, I can't imagine her being a troublemaker," I commented.

"She wasn't being a troublemaker," answered Mr. Whimple. "She ended up in detention because another girl lied to her teacher about her cheating on a test."

"Mr. Needle! How dare you give my mom detention!"

"It wasn't me! I didn't do it!"

"Oh. Well, then who did?"

"I don't know," answered Mr. Whimple. "I don't remember. Anyway, it looks like we're about to reach the bus station."

Sure enough, we did. Several minutes later, Mr. Needle paid for our bus tickets. Hurrying on the bus, I waved goodbye to Mr. Whimple. Dori and Mr. Needle were already on it.

52

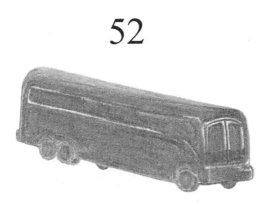

The bus ride was long. We had a rest stop every two hours. Dori listened to music most of the time while Mr. Needle read. And I slept through most of it. I was glad when we arrived.

"This way," said Mr. Needle, gesturing.

I lugged my suitcase. Dori waited with Mr. Needle on a sidewalk.

"The housing is next door to the school," said Mr. Needle. "Our rooms are already booked."

"Rooms?" I said.

"Only two rooms will be paid for. You and I will have to share. Dori gets her own room. Doesn't that sound like fun?" Elbowed Mr. Needle. "We get to be roomies."

Dori smiled.

"We won't be spending too much time in the room anyway," said Mr. Needle. "Come on, it's this way."

We walked to a gated entrance. A uniformed guard came out and confronted us. Mr. Needle handed him an ID badge.

"Nice to see you again, Mr. Needle," he said, scanning his badge. Are you here on important business."

"No, no. We're here for the indoor track and field event."

"I see. Well, have fun tomorrow." The guard handed the badge back.

A moment later he opened the gate, and we entered. Walking on a sidewalk, we came to a large, brick building.

"This is the housing area," said Mr. Needle.

Entering inside, we spotted a middle-aged woman at the front desk. She looked at us.

"It's nice to see you again, Mr. Needle. Will you be staying long?"

"Just for the annual track and field day."

"Ah, I see." She said, smiling at me and Dori. "Well, I'm sure, you'll have loads of fun."

"We plan on it," answered Mr. Needle.

"Good, and do you have rooms booked already?" she asked.

"Yes, my name should be on record."

She typed in Mr. Needle's name on a computer. "Ah, here we go. You are booked for two rooms for two nights."

"Yes."

"Okay, that will be $200.00 dollars."

Mr. Needle got out his debit card and gave it to her. A moment later, she handed it back.

"Thank you. I hope you enjoy your stay here. I'll get your room keys." She grabbed four keys off a hook and set them on the desk. "Your room numbers are 119 and 120."

Mr. Needle grabbed the keys and gave two to Dori. A minute later, we were getting settled in.

53

The next morning, we waited in a long line outside the gymnasium at the AGT academy. Before people could go in, they had to be ushered through a smaller building first. It was connected to the gym.

"Next," said a man.

I stepped up.

"Name."

"Eddie Whimple."

He searched my name on an electronic, hand-held device.

"Okay, proceed."

I hurried inside. A young man ushered me to a tall box. It reminded me of an old-fashioned telephone booth, except it had no windows.

"Please, step inside."

I entered, and he shut the door. It was pitch black on the inside. Just outside the room, there was a key pad. I heard him hit some buttons. A moment later a light came on, scanning me. After a minute, the man opened the door.

"Okay, you're good."

He ushered me out of the little room and through a door on the other side. In a daze I entered the gym. A young woman stood near the entrance. She handed me a pamphlet.

"If you have a cellphone, please turn it off." She said. "Do not have it out, or it will be confiscated. That goes for all electronic devices. For everyone's safety, please follow the rules." She motioned for me to pass.

Stepping forward, I scanned the gym. People were everywhere, moving up and down on the black bleachers. I stood there like a statue, until Dori and Mr. Needle showed up.

"You okay, Eddie," said Dori.

I nodded.

"Wow, this place is amazing!" Dori gawked. "Check out their court."

"This way," said Mr. Needle, directing us. "We need to find seats."

We hurried through the crowd. Trying to keep up, I spotted a familiar, fair-skinned girl with blond hair, coming our way. She was trying to get our attention and was waving at us.

I tapped Dori on the shoulder. "Look, it's Cindy."

Dori glanced to see.

"Hey, guys," said Cindy, rushing over. "I'm so glad you came."

"Thanks," I said. "It's good to see you."

"Are you going to show us around?" asked Dori.

"I was going to, but I have to stay with my class. I just wanted to say hi. Maybe we can do something later."

"Okay," said Dori.

Cindy then hurried back. A loud voice sounded across the gym.

"Everyone, may I please have your attention! In a few minutes, our indoor track and field will begin. If you will look at your pamphlet, it will tell you when each contest will start. So, please have a seat and enjoy."

We hurried to the bleachers.

"Now you see," said Mr. Needle, sitting down. "They start with the youngest group first and go on up. Students must demonstrate their skills through metamorphosis. If you look on your pamphlet, you will see the three listed events; running, jumping, and catching.

Dori and I sat down next to Mr. Needle.

"In the first event, students will race against each other as an animal."

"What's catching?" I asked.

"Oh, that's when a student catches a ball as a dog," answered Mr. Needle.

"Hence the name… catching," said Dori, using her fingers as quotation marks.

"Be quiet." I elbowed. "You didn't know what that meant either."

"Anyway, if they miss, it counts against them. They try to catch as many balls as they can. The longer they go, the quicker a ball is thrown."

"Cool," I said. "So, what happens if a student wins an event?"

"They win a scholarship fund award."

We watched as eight students lined up to race.

"Every year the teachers let them decide what animals they want to race as," said Mr. Needle. "For instance, the entire sixth grade can vote on racing against each other as cats or dogs. This year they picked dogs."

A second later, they transformed.

"Notice anything unusual about the students?" asked Mr. Needle.

"Yeah, all of them are different sizes," I said, staring.

There were eight different forms of dogs on the track.

"That doesn't seem fair," replied Dori. "They should all race as the same type of dog."

"They're only sixth graders," answered Mr. Needle. He paused for a moment.

"What?" asked Dori, looking at him.

"I forgot that you're only thirteen."

"Fourteen!"

Mr. Needle laughed. "Doesn't seem possible. Anyway, you and Eddie have had extra training. Still… it's not a fair race. Is it? How's that little one supposed to keep up?"

"Maybe they should have studied different dog breeds," I said. "They could have transformed into a faster dog."

"More than likely they haven't learned how to transform into different breeds yet," said Mr. Needle. "Usually first years always transform into what's most comfortable for them. Like how you would always transform into a wolf. Sometimes even when you didn't want to."

I blushed.

"The academy is really large, but there aren't many students per grade. The average graduating class is between 25 and 30 students. So, roughly between 175 and 210 students attend here, 6th through 12th grade."

"Wish I was going here." Dori sighed. "I overheard my parents talking. They're planning on sending us to a public school next year." She gave a pouty face.

"Really?" I said. "They said that?"

"Yes."

"Then that means…" I stared at Mr. Needle. "You're leaving?"

He looked at me. "Eddie, you knew it was a one-year program, and you've completed it."

I suddenly felt sad.

"When I get back to the inn, I'll have to pack my things and move on."

"What!?" cried Dori, clutching him. "Where will you go? What will you do?"

"I'm still going to continue doing the program," he said, patting her arm. "But there are other children who need training."

"It's not fair," said Dori. And she gave another pouty face.

"Dori, we're here to have fun," replied Mr. Needle. "Here." He handed her some money. "Why don't you go to the concession stand and get us something to eat? Eddie, you can go with her. It's upstairs."

54

We came back from the concession stand with hot dogs and drinks. While munching on the food, we watched the different events. It was fun to see. We rooted for Cindy. When she was done competing, she hung out with her classmates. After a while she came over to visit.

"Hey guys!" said Cindy. "May I sit?"

We scooted over.

"Are you sure you won't get in trouble?" I asked.

"My teacher said it was alright."

"Who's your teacher?" asked Dori.

"Mrs. Edaline." She pointed to a grey-haired woman on the track.

Dori's face froze. "She probably wouldn't let you sit with us if she knew who my dad was."

We burst out, laughing. Cindy looked confused.

"Inside joke," replied Mr. Needle.

"We'll tell you later," said Dori.

"So, how did you do on the other events?" I asked. "I saw that you made third in running."

"I'm not sure," said Cindy. "I didn't do as good as I wanted."

"I'm sorry."

"It's alright. Better luck next year… Hey look!" She pointed. "They're about to do the seniors. I love it when the older teens jump the hurdles. And then afterwards they do tricks for the audience."

"What do you mean?" I asked.

"Usually each senior is talented in one area of metamorphosis," explained Mr. Needle. "Whether it's performing spectacular feats with a certain animal or rapidly transitioning into animals in sequence. It's their last hurrah, so to speak. Before they go to college."

"Cool."

We watched the seniors perform their events. And then afterwards, just like Cindy mentioned, they did their tricks. It was a lot of fun to see, but soon it was over. The crowd got up to leave.

"Are you guys going to stay around?" asked Cindy.

Dori gave Mr. Needle the puppy eyes.

"We need to go back to the housing area for a little bit," said Mr. Needle. "But we can come back to the academy and have a look around."

"What time will you guys be back?" asked Cindy.

"Around two," answered Mr. Needle.

"Okay, I'll see you guys later. Don't forget to message me when you arrive." And she took off.

55

Dori messaged Cindy to let her know we were heading out. She met us in front of the academy next to an outdoor fountain.

"Well, Cindy, shall you give us the grand tour," said Mr. Needle, gesturing with his hand.

"Sure, it will be an honor," replied Cindy. She smiled and turned on her heels, walking up the steps.

We hurried to the red, brick building after her.

"The school building has automatic locks." She explained to us. "Normally they keep the building open, but classes are canceled today. Since I'm a Student TA, I have the code to get in."

"You're a Student TA?" said Dori. "I guess it makes sense, your dad is a teacher here."

"Actually, it helps toward future costs," answered Cindy.

"So, that she can earn scholarship money," explained Mr. Needle.

Cindy punched in a series of numbers and symbols, until the double doors unlocked. A moment later, we were inside. She shut the doors behind us.

We strolled down a long hallway. Lockers lined both sides. I then noticed pictures, hanging on the wall at the far end. I didn't recognize a single person, except for two. One was Cindy's father and the other...

"Hey," I said, walking up to it. "It's Mr. Needle."

"Yep," answered Cindy. She smiled and stared at a young Mr. Needle in the photo.

"Are you sure?" asked Dori, squinting. "It doesn't have Mr. Needle's round belly."

"I ought to whop you, Dori Whimple," said Mr. Needle. "You're lucky I have a good sense of humor."

"As if you'd hit an ex-student." She grinned.

"Ex-student?"

"I passed all my tests. Didn't I?"

He cocked his eyes. "I haven't left yet."

"Do I need to separate you two?" asked Cindy.

We laughed.

"Come on, let's move on," replied Mr. Needle.

We hurried past the classrooms and walked out a back exit. We came to a brick building next door. Cindy took out a card and slid it through a sliding, card lock on a door. Unlocking it, she let us in.

"This is our indoor swimming pool," said Cindy.

Several students stared at us from the pool.

"Wish I'd brought my swimsuit," commented Dori. She rolled her eyes up at Mr. Needle.

"Oops," said Mr. Needle.

We waved to the students in the water and left the building. Shortly after, Cindy pointed at the dorms along the way.

"What's that over there?" I asked.

"Oh, that's the greenhouse," said Cindy. "We can take a look in it."

We rushed over to a building with glass walls, entering inside. Two large, long tables stretched across the room. Tons and tons of plants covered the tops.

"Most of these are student projects," explained Cindy. "This one's mine." She pointed to a potted plant with purple flowers. "It's a geranium."

"Oh, and I see you're taking good care of it," commented Mr. Needle. "Do you talk to it? Mother always talked to her flowers." He added.

"Yes, sometimes," answered Cindy.

"Does it help?" I asked.

"I think so. It has something to do with carbon dioxide. It's supposed to help them grow."

"There, there, Mr. Plant," said Dori, pretending to stroke it.

"Now you're just making fun of me," said Cindy. Her hands were on her hip.

Dori stuck her tongue out.

"Anyway, I guess, we better finish up the tour," replied Cindy.

"Where to next?" asked Mr. Needle.

"Well, you've already seen the gym. How about Pucker?"

"Pucker?" I questioned.

"It's where people make weird faces," remarked Dori.

"No, it's where our concert room is held," answered Cindy. "The band and choir share it. They perform plays and musicals there."

"It's that brick building over there," said Mr. Needle, pointing.

We walked over to it. Cindy pulled out her card and unlocked the doors for us. The building was huge on the inside. It sank inward like an indoor colosseum, except the rows of chairs only covered half the room. Down at the bottom was a stage. Students sat on chairs, playing musical pieces on their instruments.

"They're getting ready for their last concert of the year," said Cindy. "The performance is next Saturday."

We watched them practice for a little bit and then exited.

"Are you guys hungry?" asked Cindy. "The cafeteria is open right now. If we hurry, we'll beat the crowd."

We rushed to a smaller building next door. Hurrying inside, we confronted a young man, running a register. Cindy slid her card through the machine.   She turned and looked at us.

"There's no reason to slide your card for us to eat," said Mr. Needle. "I have a card of my own."

He took it out and slid his card for me and Dori to pay for our food. We then hurried to a buffet table. We had a choice of burgers or pizza. There was also a salad bar. We picked out what we wanted, grabbed our drinks, and seated ourselves next to Cindy at a rectangle table. Some of her school friends joined us. They asked us a lot of questions, and we did our best to answer them. After visiting, it was time to leave.

"We have to go back to the housing area," said Dori. "Thanks for showing us around, Cindy."

"Yeah, it was a lot of fun," I replied.

"Well, for the most part," commented Dori. "It would have been better if I'd known about the indoor swimming pool." She cocked her eyes at Mr. Needle.

"Now really, Dori," said Mr. Needle. "Like you want to see an old man in a swimming pool, especially since I have a round belly."

"If you really wanted to swim," I said, looking at Dori. "We could have shoved you in."

She stuck her tongue out at me.

"Anyway, we appreciate it, Cindy," said Mr. Needle. "Thanks for the tour."

"Not a problem," answered Cindy. "I'm glad you came."

We then left the cafeteria.

56

   The next day we packed our things and left the academy. It was time to go back. Riding on the bus, I thought a lot about what happened. Being there reminded me of my old school, except it was a lot fancier than what I was used to. But seeing all the students there reminded me of my old friends. I could see why Dori wanted to go there. It was a really nice place. *Maybe the public school that Mr. and Mrs. Whimple are sending us to next year won't be so bad.* I then drifted off to sleep. I slept through most of the bus trip.

   Mr. Whimple picked us up at the bus stop and drove us home later that evening. Mrs.

Whimple confronted us. We stood in the hallway near the front desk.

"Did you guys have a good time?" she asked.

"Yeah, it was fun," said Dori. "Wish I could have brought a swimsuit though." She stared at Mr. Needle.

He wiggled his eyebrows.

"But, yeah, it was fun."

"Oh good. I wish I could have gone. Well, why don't you guys go upstairs and rest. It's pretty late. I've got some cleaning to do."

I hurried upstairs to my room. Unlocking the door, I placed my suitcase on my bed and began to unpack my things. In doing so, it suddenly occurred to me how crazy things had been, since I started living here. So many things had happened. It was just amazing how much change could occur in almost a year. Thinking about this, I got ready for bed.

The following day I walked out of my room to see Mr. Needle coming down the hall. He was carrying two suitcases.

"Mr. Needle?" I said.

"I've come to say goodbye," he answered, setting his suitcases down.

"Already?"

"Yes, I have to go to a different state. I… wanted to give you this." He pulled something out of his pocket. "I was going to give it to you on your birthday." He handed it to me.

An object was wrapped in newspaper. I unraveled it. Inside it was a hand carved wolf.

"I know how much you like wolves," he said. "May it be a reminder for you."

My eyes welled.

"Don't forget what I taught you." He touched my shoulder. "Keep practicing. I'm going to say goodbye to the rest of the family now."

I stopped him, picking up one of his suitcases. He allowed me to take it, and I followed him down the stairs. The family was waiting at the front desk. But a shocked expression crossed Dori's face.

"You're leaving now?"

"I have to."

Dori nodded. She then rushed over and gave him a hug.

"Promise me you'll come back for a visit."

Mr. Needle smiled. "Just hang on to your fat panther. Hopefully, we'll see each other again someday."

Dori let go. And we escorted him out to his car, helping him put his suitcases in his trunk. A moment later he hopped in his car, waving goodbye.

Goodbye, Mr. Needle. I said, telepathically.

Goodbye, Eddie. May you have many more adventures.

The End